MW00941223

YOU, ME, AND THE STARS

ALSO BY
MICHELLE DYKMAN

Her Sanctuary, His Heart

The Deal with Dakota

If Only In My Dreams

Someone Like You
BETHEL PRIVATE SCHOOL SERIES | BOOK TWO

MICHELLE DYKMAN

BETHEL PRIVATE SCHOOL SERIES | BOOK ONE

Ambassador International
GREENVILLE, SOUTH CAROLINA & BELFAST, NORTHERN IRELAND

www.ambassador-international.com

YOU, ME, AND THE STARS

©2021 by Michelle Dykman
All rights reserved

ISBN: 978-1-64960-107-0
eISBN: 978-1-64960-157-5
Library of Congress Control Number: 2021941497

Cover design by Hannah Linder Designs
Interior Typesetting by Dentelle Design
Digital Edition by Anna Riebe Raats
Edited by Megan Gerig

No part of this publication may be reproduced, distributed, or transmitted in any form or by any means, including photocopying, recording, or other electronic or mechanical methods, without the prior written permission of the publisher, except in the case of brief quotations embodied in critical reviews and certain other noncommercial uses permitted by copyright law. For permission requests, contact the publisher using the information below.

This is a work of fiction. Names, characters, and incidents are all products of the author's imagination or are used for fictional purposes. Any resemblance to actual events or persons, living or dead, is entirely coincidental. Any mentioned brand names, places, and trademarks remain the property of their respective owners, bear no association with the author or the publisher, and are used for fictional purposes only.

Scripture taken from the Holy Bible, New International Version®, NIV® Copyright ©1973, 1978, 1984, 2011 by Biblica, Inc.® Used by permission. All rights reserved worldwide.

AMBASSADOR INTERNATIONAL
Emerald House
411 University Ridge, Suite B14
Greenville, SC 29601, USA
www.ambassador-international.com

AMBASSADOR BOOKS
The Mount
2 Woodstock Link
Belfast, BT6 8DD, Northern Ireland, UK
www.ambassadormedia.co.uk

The colophon is a trademark of Ambassador, a Christian publishing company.

DEDICATION

All glory and honor to the Lord for giving me the inspiration to write this book. To my hubby, your unfailing belief in me has given me the courage to leap into the unknown. To the special teens that inspired this book, you guys are one in a million. God bless you all.

PREFACE

High school reminds us of the things that used to be. Dreams that have never been realized. Dreams shattered by some bad choice or decision. Dreams given to the young and then painfully jerked away when reality set in. We all had dreams once, things we would achieve, places we would go, and a picture of a very different life than the one we may have now. There is always a reason a dream dies, reality crushing it until there is nothing left but an echo, a whisper, or maybe a gasp. Sometimes dreams are revived but only after some hard life lessons have been learned. This is where we find ourselves looking back at our dreams.

"He has made everything beautiful in its time. He has also set eternity in the human heart; yet no one can fathom what God has done from beginning to end."

Ecclesiastes 3:11

ONE

"Remind me why I took this class again?" Willow groaned.

"Because you need a science requirement for college," Felicia retorted.

"Right, and why do I want to go to college?"

Felicia snorted and leaned back in her chair. "Cute boys."

Willow flashed an exaggerated wink in this week's date's direction as she sat down and pulled out her mirror. Her hair and lips would need some attention after their earlier passionate interlude. She ran her tongue over her bruised lips before sliding her favorite strawberry lip gloss over them. Brad was an okay kisser but magic with his hands. She could find a better kisser next week. Every boy in Bethel Private School wanted a chance to tame Wild Willow.

She smirked and applied another layer of her pink lip gloss and ran her hands through her tangled hair. She needed a brush.

Felicia plopped into the desk next to her. "You still up for a rager this weekend? My folks are visiting my aunt again."

"Class, settle down," Mrs. Wilson called.

"What drinks?" Willow whispered.

Felicia thought for a minute. "I can ask Jace's older brother if he'll go to the bottle store for us again. Those Trailblazers and Fruity mishmash's we made last time were good. Although maybe Jace could. His birthday is on Friday."

"Who's coming? Hang on a sec. Let me text the guys." Willow whipped out her phone and opened the group chat app.

Felicia leaned over her desk. "Add Brady."

Willow nodded. She didn't how she'd make that one fly. Oh well. Brady or Brad. She'd choose later.

"Ms. Rysen and Ms. Wren, please keep your discussions for after school." Mrs. Wilson gave them both a stern look.

Willow smiled sweetly and clicked off her phone. She didn't need another trip to Principal Rory's office this week. Good thing Daddy had paid for the renovations on the library last year.

"Today, I will be assigning you partners for your final science project." Mrs. Wilson cleared her throat and ran her finger down the paper on her desk. "Felicia Wren, you will be going with Ted Martin."

Willow focused on making a party list. She didn't care who she got. She'd make them do the work and sail off their grade. The nerdy types were always ready and willing to help the Queen Bee of Bethel just for a special mention on her lips. Willow smiled. It was so easy to be her.

The period bled on. Willow finished the party list and started doodling around the names. She curled roses up and over their names before drawing several sets of large spikes on the roses' stems. The party list soon resembled a thorny rose garden bursting with luscious lips. Willow couldn't help remembering Brad's lips from this morning. So soft and kissable. Connor caught her eye. She smiled. Maybe she should give Connor another go. He was a better kisser. She scribbled his name onto the list.

Someone shook her arm. Willow glanced over at Felicia and raised an eyebrow. "Huh?"

"You're paired with some guy named Christian Blythe."

"Who's that?" She scanned the room, hoping to see a new face that could maybe be her mysterious science partner, but the same old faces filled her vision. Amy Carter sat next to Felicia. Brad and his friends goofed off in the far corner, and the social misfits sat around trying not to be noticed by anybody. Christian was most likely in the other class. She shrugged and returned to her drawings.

"At Bethel we hold to Christian ideologies and truths; however, in secular circles, it is said that science and the Bible can in no way complement each other," Mrs. Wilson said. "We are going to look at this subject and discuss it from a Christian and a non-Christian perspective. You and your partner will each take a side, and in one month's time, you will present your project to the class in the form of a debate."

Snorting, Willow rolled her eyes and crossed her arms with practiced impatience over her chest. Great! She would have to do some of the project. This day had just gone from easy to a cataclysmic disaster.

"Will." Felicia tapped her desk, throwing her attention back to the classroom.

Mrs. Wilson was still talking. Maybe she should pay attention. Heaven knew she needed this grade.

"Wikipedia, is not a valid source, so don't even try it." Mrs. Wilson glanced in Amy's direction.

Amy's face broke out in a red river, and Willow smirked. She took out her nail file and studied her nails. Neither side of the argument sounded particularly appealing. Her father had once said that Christians were the reason the world was in such a mess. She'd choose the side with the least amount of work.

Just as she reached her last fingernail, the bell rang and freed her from giving any other thought to her science class. Willow grabbed her bag and stuffed her notebook and the assignment sheet in before swinging it over her shoulder and making for the door. She'd look at it later if she was bored and had nothing better to do with her time.

Felicia linked arms with her, and they strolled to their next class. "Any idea who this guy is?"

"I hope he's hot and athletic."

Felicia laughed then pulled to a stop. "Watch—"

Willow smacked into something hard. She stumbled back, a strong hand wrapping around her wrist to stop her fall.

"Sorry, are you all right?" a quiet voice like smooth melted chocolate over a cold ice cream asked. Delicious.

Willow opened her mouth to speak, then her words froze in her throat as the owner of the voice came into view. Dark hair curled around the boy's angular face, and soft brown eyes that could melt your heart peeked out from behind black fashionable glasses. And his lips. Those lips were made for kissing.

The boy cleared his throat, a faint pink in his cheeks, and extended his hand toward her. "Hi, I'm Christian Blythe."

Willow smiled and shook the boy's hand. So, this was her science partner. "Willow Rysen." Little tingles traveled up her arm from where their hands connected. Working with this guy was going to be something to remember.

"Will, we have to go. The smell of nerd is offending my nose," Felicia said.

"What?" Willow yanked her gaze away from Christian's face, taking note of what he wore in one hurried swoop. Baggie cargo pants, an open blue button up, and an orange t-shirt that said, "I learned to speak Klingon." Nerd indeed.

Willow sneered. The giddy feeling she'd had a moment ago turning into abject horror. She glared at Christian. How dare he? Ignoring the clear disbelief in his expression, she dragged Felicia around him and stormed off to their next class, silently cursing the butterflies that still fluttered in her tummy.

What was going on with her?

Shaking her head, she pushed back her shoulders and plastered a bogusly happy smile on her face. "So, that party on Saturday."

TWO

Christian stared after Willow and Felicia. He whistled under his breath and checked his arms and legs. All still attached. For a moment, he hadn't believed the rumors about Willow could possibly be true, but the change that had come over Willow's expression when she saw his clothes would melt even the staunchest soldier's spine. He ran his hand through his hair, thankful he'd walked away with his life. Working with Willow was bound to be fraught with peril. So much for the hours and hours of work he and Jack had slaved away this summer looking for the perfect senior science experiment. All that work was now for nothing. How could Mrs. Wilson do this to him?

"Willow Rysen, man, why do you have all the luck?" Jack stopped beside Christian, his gaze focused on the two girls walking away from them.

"You call this lucky?" Christian gestured ahead of them. "I'll be lucky if I survive the month. What could you possibly see in a girl like that?"

"She's stunning and those legs. The stuff dreams are made of."

"Come on, man. A nice pretty package with the tongue of a viper. I think I'll pass."

Jack frowned, his eyebrows scrunched in the way he looked when something obvious occurred to him. Christian paused. Long chestnut hair with a soft curl, bright blue eyes, and killer body—Willow was truly every teenage boy's fantasy girl. If he hadn't heard the vitriol that came pouring out of those pouty lips, he might be drawn in just like Jack.

"Look around you, Jack, any girl would be better than Willow." Christian clamped his hand on Jack's shoulder, swinging his attention in the opposite direction. "Go use that teddy bear charm on someone who'll appreciate it."

"Perhaps." Jack's gaze landed on a girl struggling with her locker a few meters away from them. A ghost of a smile formed on his mouth. Glancing quickly at Christian, he threw a "what can you do?" shrug and went over to help her.

Good old Jack. If there was a damsel in distress, Jack couldn't help himself. He would do everything in his power to help her. Since his earliest memory of Jack, Christian hadn't met a person more loyal or giving as his giant of a friend.

Frowning, Christian watched Willow and Felicia disappear around the corner. This was totally messed up. There was no way he and Willow could work together, but he needed this grade. Mind muddling over how he was going to make this work, Christian walked to his next class. Hopefully, he'd think of something. Maybe he could beg Mrs. Wilson for a new partner.

By the time Christian drove home, he'd bit his tongue more times than he could count. His mom had taught him how to speak to a lady, but after Willow's stream of snarky comments throughout the day, his ability to be a gentleman had just about run out.

"Rough day?" His mom walked down the hall toward him.

"You know that science project Jack and I were working on? Well, Mrs. Wilson partnered me with the worst possible person. I am probably going to fail science now."

His mom's eyes went wide. "It can't be that bad."

"Mom, she partnered me with the nastiest girl in the school. Ms. Popular, Spoiled Brat Willow Rysen." As soon as the words left his mouth, he wanted to swallow them back.

"Christian," his mom's hand came to rest on his tense shoulder, "all your life I've tried to teach you to see the best in people and to be the best person you can be. Willow may be a lot of things, but maybe she needs you to show her how to be a better person. Sometimes God gives us tasks that seem impossible, and without Him, they are. Do you want to pray about it?"

Christian shook his head. He needed some air. "I think I'll go to Games and Things. I'll be back before dinner."

His mom gave him a sad smile, but she nodded. "Okay. Know that I'll be praying for you."

Christian grabbed his car keys and slid his favorite CD into the car player, a heavy drumbeat pounding the interior. He sang along as he drove to the mall, but for once, the song didn't ease the tension inside of him. Man, this was worse than he thought.

The parking garage was emptier than it would have been on a Friday night, and he easily found a parking spot. Closing the door and pressing the locks, he slid his keys and wallet into his back pocket and walked toward the closest entrance, his mind fixed on the impossibility of his current dilemma.

"Hey watch—" A body of shopping bags crashed into him and bounced back, landing in an untidy heap on the shiny mall floor. He stumbled, caught his balance, and looked down, amusement pushing past his anger.

"Watch where you're going, buddy," came a venomous squawk from inside the pile.

Christian flushed. "Sorry, I didn't see you there. Let me help." He reached down to aid the girl while trying his best to suppress the wave of laughter that threatened to spill out.

Willow's outraged face emerged from in between the mountain of shopping bags. Christian lost the battle, and bellows of laughter surged out of him, echoing around them.

"Are you following me?" he gasped, succumbing to another wave of laughter.

Willow flushed a deep crimson, her pouty lips pressed into a hard line. Her eyes sparkled and a small curve fought its way across her mouth.

"You ran into me remember? So, you must be following me." She grabbed his proffered hand and pushed to her feet, wearing a wry smile.

Still chuckling, Christian collected the scattered purchases and handed them one by one to her. "Well, seeing as we're both standing here, maybe we could discuss our science project?"

All hilarity disappeared from Willow's face. Her expression pinched. Grabbing Christian by the hand, she towed him into an alley between two stores. "Let's get one thing straight here, Mr. Goody Two Shoes. I don't do projects with ugly people. In fact, I don't want anything to do with a guy like you. So, you do the project, I'll sign my name, and that's that."

The anger he'd tried so hard to suppress came roaring back to the surface. He crossed his arms. "Not going to happen, sweet cheeks.

Either you do this project with me or I speak to Mrs. Wilson and Principal Rory."

Willow's face pale, a hint of something shining in those gorgeous blue eyes. "Fine." Impatience hummed through that one small word.

Christian waited and slid his hands into his pockets. It was her choice. "Meet me in the geography section in the library at six p.m. tonight."

"No." She glared at him and arched an eyebrow in a challenge. "I have a date tonight, and I'm certainly not cancelling for you."

Christian blinked. On a school night? Didn't people date on the weekends? Not that he would know. "Okay, tomorrow night, same place, same time?"

Willow scowled but nodded. "Whatever." She scooped up her shopping bags, threw one more disgusted look at him, and stormed out of the alley.

What had just happened? Had he entered some weird second dimension? He looked around him. No, he was still at the mall, still in the same alley she'd dragged him into. Running his hand down his face, he blew out a deep breath. His gaze landing on something small near the entrance of the alley. A white bag. No doubt one of Willow's shopping bags. Christian grimaced. "Oh boy."

THREE

Willow slammed the trunk of her red Beamer closed. Thank goodness that was over. She wished she could swap partners, but Mrs. Wilson always preferred the nerds in her class. And if Mrs. Wilson involved Principal Rory. . .Irritation lanced through her. She didn't have time for this.

Pushing all thoughts of science and Christian aside, Willow drove home, her mind already turning to her upcoming date. Humming to the music playing, she smiled as she thought of Brad. His deep blue eyes, velvety voice, and those lips that could make her forget her own name. Just the pick-me-up she needed after her horrible encounter with that other boy. Feeling more upbeat, she gathered her bags and hurried into the house.

An hour later, she stood in front of the mirror, styled and ready to go. She admired the way her red dress highlighted her sleek and hard-earned shape. Thank you, Zumba classes. One more sweep of strawberry lip gloss, and she was ready to go. She grabbed a deep blue coat and slid it onto her shoulders, lamenting the cold weather.

"Are you going out tonight?" her mom asked.

Willow paused on the bottom step. "Yeah."

Her mother took a deep breath. "Don't you have homework?"

"No." She had a ton, but her mother didn't need to know that.

Her mother watched her for a long moment. Willow stood silent. The tension in the room mounted. This was how it always was in their house. The silent battle of wills between her and her mother. And her father on the rare occasions he was home. They weren't a family. They were just three people that lived under the same roof. Willow suppressed the pang of longing that always followed one of these encounters. Her life was what it was.

Willow pulled her gaze from her mother's questioning eyes and walked out the door. She stopped briefly under the porch light to gather her emotions. Brad's car waited at the bottom of the driveway like it always did on date night. Willow burrowed deeper into her coat, briskly rubbing her hands together. Forget her mom. It was time to focus on date night. The interior light of the car flickered on, and she slid into the passenger side.

"Hey." Brad shot her a smile, but it didn't seem as magical as usual.

She cocked her head. "Brad, what's up?"

He frowned and shrugged a muscled shoulder. "Nothing. Denny's or the Hilltop?"

Willow studied the slump of Brad's shoulder and the droop of his smile. "What is going on with you tonight?"

"Nothing," he snapped and shifted the gear into drive. "Let's go to Denny's."

Willow adjusted her hands on her lap. He'd never used that tone with her before. Nerves fluttered in her stomach, and they weren't the good kind.

Denny's came into view, and Brad pulled the car to a stop, but he didn't move. In fact, he hadn't said a word the entire drive.

"Brad, are you sure you're okay? Or do I need to use more drastic measures to get you to talk?" She slid her hand over his thigh and scooted closer to him.

Brad turned to face her, his strong arm locking behind her shoulders and drawing her closer. The kiss seemed almost mechanical with an edge of anger mixed with desperation. And those magic hands had not moved from behind her shoulders.

Willow pulled back. "Brad, what's going on? Your head isn't here."

Brad's expression darkened. "Sorry, I'm just going through some stuff right now." A hardness was in his voice.

"What stuff?" she huffed. A date was not the time to go through "some stuff."

"Like you care."

Willow shrugged. She didn't care, but she wasn't about to admit that. Closing the space between them, she pressed her lips onto his again, willing him to forget whatever was bugging him.

He kissed her a few moments then thrust her back into her seat. "I can't do this." Brad shifted away from her and pressed his head back into the head rest, his jaw clenching and unclenching in time with his tapping fingers.

"Do what? Make out? You didn't seem to have any problem with it this morning."

Brad was silent for a long time, then he finally said, "You know what, Willow, I've had enough of being your plaything. I'm done."

Willow pursed her lips. She clasped her shaking hands in her lap. Was he breaking up with her? "Well, thank goodness for that. I don't know how much longer I could put up with your whining."

Brad grimaced and started the car. "Figures."

He raced back to her house where she hopped out of the car and slammed the door shut without saying goodbye. Her heart pounded in her chest, and she sucked in a few deep breaths. What did she care? Brad was just another one in the long list of losers. She didn't need him. After all, she wasn't called Wild Willow for nothing. She pulled out her phone, barely past seven. Maybe she'd go to the library after all and get all the unpleasant experiences over with in one night. Christian would probably be there, the nerd that he was.

Chuckling quietly, she slipped back into the house. After taking a few minutes to change, she made for the door again. A creak on the stairs turned her around, her mother stood on the second-floor landing looking down at her, her question clear.

"I'm going out." Flinging her schoolbag over her shoulder, Willow walked out into the night for the second time that evening.

A short while later, Willow found herself outside the public library, debating whether she wanted to go in. Christian's threat still hung over her. She didn't really have a choice. If there was an option between spending time in the library or detention, the library looked like the better choice. "You can do this." She shoved the heavy wooden doors aside and walked in.

"Can I help you dear?" An elderly lady asked behind a wooden reception area. She scanned the bar codes from a stack of books piled beside her then carefully placed the book on a neat heap beside her.

"Yes, please, can you tell me where the geography section is?" Willow asked. Her face flushed at the question. She didn't know anything about a library. Who needed the library when there was the internet?

The lady lifted her hand to direct her just as Christian came around the corner. Willow's breath caught. What was wrong with her tonight? He walked toward her, a stack of books in one hand and a takeout cup of coffee in his other. Christian froze and his eyes widened. Finally, he cleared his throat and said, "I didn't expect to see you here tonight. What about your date?"

"Big bust." She smiled, pleased she'd decided to come.

Christian's mouth quirked up at the side, the relief in his expression almost funny.

"Any chance there's another one of those somewhere?" she asked, gesturing to the coffee.

"Ah, no. I haven't drank from this one so your welcome to it."

"Really?"

"I have a bottle of water. This way. I got a table in the back. Remind me later to get something you left at the mall. I have it in my car."

Willow scanned the room as she walked. Lines and lines of shelves stood in every direction, and yellow light that shone from the roof gaze a peaceful glow. It was so different from the bright lights that they had at school. So much cozier. A strange smell, unfamiliar but nice filled her nose and she wondered what it was.

Turning her gaze forward, Willow studied Christian. He had a confident gait and was just the right height for her tastes. His dark hair rested on the top collar of his plaid shirt, and even though she detested chino pants, they did look great on him. Willow snorted in dismay at her thoughts. Whoa, girl, not ever. But there was nothing wrong with looking.

Christian turned and raised an eyebrow. She waved him off with a small smile then stumbled when an answering smile flicked across his lips. She dropped her gaze down to her heeled boots in disgust. *Where's your head at, Willow?*

Finally, Christian came to a stop at a large wooden table. "You can take that seat if you like?" he said. She took a seat opposite him and threw her bag onto top of table. His laptop was already open, and he had some old books lying next to him. He'd obviously been here for a while. Willow sat down, took a sip of the warm coffee, and pulled out her nail file. Christian grimaced. Then she took out her phone and scrolled through her messaging app.

"Willow, is this your idea of working together? Me working and you doing whatever you're doing?"

Willow nodded, enjoying the annoyed look on his face. She couldn't help but admire the way his hair flopped around his angry face. "Why should I do any work when you're doing such an admirable job by yourself?"

Christian's mouth settled in a firm line. "Do you even care about getting a good grade?"

Willow shrugged. "I just need a passing grade." Wasn't that obvious?

"What about the future, Willow? What are you going to do after high school?" Was it just her or did he sound condescending?

Willow shrugged again. Why did he care? "I don't know. Something I guess."

Christian's expression became puzzled. "Then why are you here?"

"Because I have to be."

His frown dipped deeper, then he shook his head and shifted his focus onto his computer again, tapping the mouse pad with obvious impatience.

Willow gazed around the room, her phone and nail file forgotten. What was she doing here?

Christian continued his typing in silence, glancing up at her every now and then. His expression grew more and more puzzled with each look. "Look, there is a speaker coming to my parent's church next week. He's doing a talk on God and science. We could go, listen, make notes, and then this will all be over. I know you don't want to work with me anymore than I want to work with you. If we do this, then we don't need to spend the next month in each other's company."

Despite how she might feel about Christian, it sounded like a good idea. She could get her grade and be done with Christian Blythe and the strange way she felt around him.

"You a church boy, Christian?" she asked.

Christian snorted but didn't answer. "Next Saturday, meet me at the Hallelujah Gospel Church on Finch road at seven p.m. I'm sure that phone of yours can help you get there." He pointed flippantly at the device resting on the table between them then turned back to his computer and effectively ended their conversation.

Willow bristled. Who did this guy think he was? "Okay, I'll go to your dumb talk, and then I don't have to be subjected to your company."

"Please do me the favor." *Was that sarcasm?*

"Whatever."

"If you don't pitch, I will tell Mrs. Wilson and Principal Rory." The hardness in his voice sounded forced.

"I said I'd be there." She rolled her eyes and grabbed her bag. "Can I go now?"

"Yeah, whatever. Don't let the door knock you on the way out," Christian ground out. If he clenched his jaw any harder, she was sure his teeth would crack.

Annoyed with his highhanded manner, she stormed out of the library.

"Wait, Willow," Christian called out.

Stopping her angry march, she squeezed the bridge of her nose. "What?"

"Your package." Christian strode past her and pushed open the heavy door. He rushed over to a blue truck, opening and slamming the heavy door before turning back to her. He handed her the small package.

She pulled it from his hand.

"You're welcome." Then he blew past her back into the library.

Willow climbed into her car and leaned her head back on the head rest. Why did her blood boil each time she encountered Christian Blythe? Who did he think he was demanding anything from her? Smacking her hand against the steering wheel, she growled in frustration and gunned for home.

FOUR

It must be Saturday night. Christian glared at the house next door. Felicia Wren, Willow's best friend, was throwing one of her infamous parties again. The loud thud of the bass drum rolled through the windows and drowned out whatever Jack had been saying on the other end of the headset. A large flash of blue flame engulfed his avatar.

Christian growled and pressed the pause button. He grabbed his phone and sent a quick text to Jack, "Hang on a minute. Felicia's at it again and I can't hear." He threw the game controller onto his bed then slammed his window shut to keep out the noise. Willow was probably next door right now. He rubbed his hands over his face. They had nothing in common and were hemispheres apart at school. Why couldn't he get her out of his mind?

"You wanna call it a night?" Jack asked when Christian slipped his headphones back on.

"Yeah, I guess. It doesn't sound like this is gonna let up any time soon."

"Cool. Check you tomorrow."

Switching off the game, Christian wandered around his room. So what if Willow was next door? What did it matter?

Maybe he was hungry. He hurried downstairs and opened the fridge. Butter, meat, pickles. A small sandwich might do it. A loud drum roll burst through the kitchen and rattled the glasses in the drying rack. Had his mom purposely opened all the windows in the house before leaving? He reached over to close the window. A shrill cry pierced the night. He stopped, the pickle jar dropping from his hand and clattering on the counter. Its wet contents splattered all over countertop.

The scream came again, louder this time. Christian flew out the back door and through the boundary line of ferns. In a dark corner of Felicia's yard, a man and a woman tussled in the grass. The man pinned the woman's wrists tightly above her head with his one hand and pawed at her dress with the other. The woman screamed again and struggled to free herself. Anger seethed into Christian. He bent low and ran at full speed, taking the man to the ground in a solid tackle then springing back to his feet with an agility that surprised even him.

The man wobbled to his feet and raised his fists. Christian tensed, his muscles rigid. The woman whimpered to his left. Christian's heart stalled and stuttered at the sight of a very pale Willow looking back up at him. Her dark brown hair was in a wild disarray, and her blue eyes shone with fear. Her face was wet with tears, and her body trembled. A surge of fierce protectiveness thrashed through him.

He faced her attacker just as the man swung at him. Christian ducked to the side, and the man drunkenly stumbled sideways. He was an easy target. Christian swung his fist, connecting solidly with the man's face in a satisfying thud. The man toppled over backward. Christian watched him, his breaths heaving out of his chest, but the man didn't move. And probably wouldn't be moving anytime soon.

Christian knelt next to Willow and reached toward her. "You're safe now. It's okay."

Willow flinched. She grabbed at her torn dress, a fresh wave of tears streaming down her face.

Christian whipped his sweatshirt over his head and handed it to her. "Here, put this on."

She slid the sweatshirt over her head and threaded her arms through the sleeves. Then she wrapped her arms around her stomach.

"Are you all right?" He took her cold hands and rubbed them between his.

Willow stared back at him her eyes wide. She blinked then blinked again.

The need to hold and protect her almost overwhelmed him, but he shook it off. This was Willow. The girl who hated him. But still, no girl should have to go through what she did.

"Can you get up?" Christian asked.

Willow nodded, and using his hand as leverage, stood shakily to her feet. Her knees gave way, and she fell against him. Christian slid his arms around her and swung her up, marching toward the back door of his house. Her soft hair brushed his cheek, and she pressed her wet cheek against his neck. Her body trembled as silent tears ran onto his shirt.

"Shh, Willow, it's all right. You're all right," Christian whispered, his anger burning at the man in a heap behind them.

The back door of his house swung open, his mother silhouetted by the light of the living room.

"Take her to the guest room," she said.

Christian nodded and followed her to the room two doors down from his. She swung the door open, ushering Christian inside.

He placed Willow on the bed, untangling her tight hold from around his neck, and took a step back. Willow's usually proud figure crumbled with sorrow onto the clean sheets.

His mom glanced at him and then swept over to the bed. "What happened?"

"A party gone wrong."

His mother nodded, her face filled with compassion. "What's your name, honey?"

When Willow didn't answer, Christian did. "Willow." He slid his clenched fists into the pockets of his jeans, struggling to suppress the anger beating in his chest. What was she thinking going outside with a guy like that? And drunk? Didn't the girl have any sense?

His mom hugged Willow gently. "Willow, my name is Susan. I'm Christian's mom. Do you want to tell me what happened?"

Willow shook her head and shivered, clutching Christian's sweatshirt to her chest. She sniffed and furiously wiped at her eyes.

A gentle smile lit his mother's face—the same smile she wore every time he got hurt when he was little. It was familiar and comforting for more than him it seemed.

"Willow, why don't you go and take a shower?" His mom glanced at Christian. "Please go downstairs and get a t-shirt and pair of sweats for her."

Christian hesitated and leaned against the door frame. They should phone the cops. "Mom—"

"Now, Christian."

He clenched his jaw and nodded. There was no use arguing when his mom used that tone. Reluctantly, he left. Busy thoughts ran through his head as he hurried down the stairs, getting what he came for and running back up. The sooner she showered, the sooner she could leave. He didn't want her here where all she did was create confusion. He paused in the doorway listening to his mom say, "Here let me." His mom lifted the sweater up over Willow's head, untangling the wild chestnut mass with care. Again, bewilderment plagued him.

"Can I come in?" he asked.

"Sure, we're just about ready here."

In the light of the guest room, the dark fingerprints on Willow's arms and wrists stood out glaringly against the creamy white of her skin. If he hadn't reached Willow in time . . . Christian shuddered and pushed any what-if scenarios out of his mind. Protectiveness clouded his thoughts. He took a step toward Willow, stopping himself from reaching out to her just in time. What was going on with him? Willow meant nothing to him. Didn't she?

Willow and his mom disappeared into the bathroom, taking his offering and closing the door. The melodious sound of his mother's voice could be heard in between the drizzle of the shower and the sobs that broke out again. He was at the door before he could stop his feet.

"Is everything all right?" he asked. Why did he care?

"She's fine. We'll be out soon," his mom answered.

He flopped back down on his perch at the end of the bed. Was Willow really okay? Had he reached her in time? What if she really was hurt? He flipped his phone in his hands, debating about calling the cops again.

The soft snick of the door caused Christian to jump to his feet and spin around. Willow stood next to his mother, her arm protectively wrapped around Willow's waist. Why did he wish it was his instead? Her wet hair hung in a loose braid on her shoulder, and her face was scrubbed clean.

He sank back down onto the bed. Willow was beautiful with makeup plastered on, but fresh-faced and innocent-looking Willow took his breath away. He couldn't keep his eyes off her.

"Are you okay?" he asked. The question sounded dumb even to him. How could someone be okay after what had happened to her?

Willow lifted one shoulder. "I think so." Breaking his stare, Willow shifted. "Susan, would you please give me a minute with Christian?" She spoke in voice that he was sure he'd never heard come out of her mouth. It was soft and gentle.

His mother glanced between the two of them before nodding. "I'll make us some tea." She bustled out of the room.

They stood in silence, awkwardly watching each other as the seconds ticked by.

"I, ah, wanted to say thank you for rescuing me." Willow slowly slid her wet braid between two fingers.

"You're welcome. Did you know that guy?" Giving into the need to be closer to her, he stepped forward. Just close enough to smell her clean, enticing scent.

"I just met him tonight."

"Did Felicia invite him?" He didn't know why he asked the question and didn't know why he cared what the answer would be.

"I think so. Felicia knows a lot of older guys because of Alex."

Something white and hot blazed through Christian. Alex, Felicia's older brother, was home from his latest tour. Christian knew it wasn't Alex's fault that his sister was what she was. What Willow was. "Do you remember how you ended up outside with him?"

Willow shuddered. "Maybe we should go and get that tea. I'm sure Susan, er, your mom has it ready by now."

The two of them walked side by side back down the stairs to the kitchen. As their hands brushed for a moment, fire raced up Christian's arm into his chest. Disguising his gasp by clearing his throat, he took a step further a way from Willow. Hopefully, the spark bouncing between them would go away. He wasn't going to start caring about Willow.

FIVE

"Do you take milk and sugar in your tea, Willow?" Susan tapped the sugar bowl with a wet teaspoon.

"I don't know. I don't usually drink tea." Mom and Dad drank only coffee. Coffee kept the brain vigilant and the thoughts pumping they said.

Christian's mom looked appalled, and Willow felt a small smile tug the side of her mouth.

"Well, then, let's put them in, and if you don't like them, I'll just make you another cup." She filled a mug for Willow then handed it to her.

The cup warmed Willow's fingers. She closed her eyes and took a sip, savoring the warm, fruity taste that spread through her. It was actually good. Not as bitter as coffee and the sweet scent somehow soothed her jumbled emotions. "It's pretty good. Thank you."

Christian snickered softly beside her and grabbed his own cup. The smell of something strong and pungent swept under Willow's nose.

Susan sat across from her with her own mug. "Would you like me to take you to the hospital or the police station?"

Willow stared down at her hands, flashes of dancing with Ethan and taking drink after drink with him circled in her memory. She didn't remember how they got outside. "No," she whispered, "I just want to forget about it. Nothing happened. Christian got there in time." She set down her cup and pushed herself to her feet. She just wanted this whole horrible night to be over.

"Willow . . . " The teacup rattled as Christian set it down. He rested his hand on her shoulder. "Maybe you should consider going to the police. What he did was wrong." His voice was so earnest, so caring that another bolt of something fluttered in her stomach. It was almost like he cared.

Scoffing at her ridiculous thoughts, Willow stepped away from Christian. "No, I—I need to get home." At home, no one would know her shame.

Susan came around and wrapped an arm around Willow's waist. "You are in no condition to drive home. You're welcome to stay as our guest for the night."

"No, I don't want to be any trouble. I think I've caused . . . " the rest of her argument disappeared at the faint hardening of Christian's mouth. His eyebrow raised in challenge. Willow sighed. "Okay. I need to send Felicia a text. I was going to spend the night at her house."

"Good. Get some sleep then. Both of you." Susan tugged Willow back up to the guest room.

Christian followed, his presence pressing into her. Even though there was at least four feet of space separating them, she knew exactly where he was. Why was that?

Susan busied herself pulling back the covers and fluffing the pillow. "If you need anything, my room is at the end of the hall. Good night, Willow." Susan's parting words followed her out of the room.

Christian braced his shoulder against the door frame, his gaze fixed on her. He opened his mouth a few times before finally murmuring, "I'm glad I got there in time."

Her stomach dipped. "Me, too," she said, purposely turning away from those soft eyes. "Good night, Christian."

"Good night, Willow." With one last smile, he walked out of the room.

Rubbing her hands over her mouth to stifle another yawn, she curled up under the covers. She stared at her phone, toying with what to say. Felicia was probably passed out by now anyway. She'd do it later. With one last yawn, she lay her head down and was out like a light.

Nausea pushed Willow out of a dead sleep. Slapping her hand over her mouth, she climbed out of bed and opened the nearest door, silently thanking her stars that it was bathroom. Lunging for the toilet, she emptied the contents of her stomach into the bowl, heaving until she was spent. Of course, tonight would come with a price. Why did she keep doing this to herself?

A minute later, white light flooded the bathroom temporarily rendering her blind.

"Willow, are you okay?" Christian stood at the door, his expression worried. His gaze darted from her to the toilet. "Oh."

"Go away," she choked out. Her humiliation was complete. Christian would never unsee her like this. Why did it matter?

Christian only stepped further into the bathroom. "It's okay." He gathered her hair in his hands, brushing it away from her face. The gesture was kind and soothing and something she knew she didn't deserve.

Willow's stomach lurched again, although there was nothing more to come. The air stank with the sour smell of alcohol. What a mess.

Strong hands lifted her to her feet and leaned her against the sink beside the toilet. Her head spun. She blinked and stiffened her legs. The last thing she wanted to do was pass out.

Christian placed a wet washcloth in her hand then guided her hand to her face. How she wished she could see past the ambivalence in his expression.

"You must think I'm so dumb," she whispered.

Christian made an impatient sound and shook his head. "A little careless but not dumb. Why do you do it?"

Willow shrugged then wobbled, slapping her hand down on the basin for support. "I don't know. It seems like fun at the time and everyone else does it. I guess I'm expected to and so I do."

Christian sighed. "That does sound dumb."

"I know." Saying it out loud made it sound more so.

"Are you okay to stand?"

Willow silently nodded, wishing the ground would swallow her up. She took one last swipe on her clammy face and braced her feet. The nausea was gone, but her stomach still rolled.

Christian exchanged the washcloth for a toothbrush then headed back out the door. "There's toothpaste in the cupboard."

Closing her eyes, Willow brushed her teeth. She had to get out of here before she did anything else to disgrace herself tonight. Staring at her reflection in the dully lit mirror, a strange emotion swept over her. It felt bad and guilty, and it was not what she wanted to feel.

"You done?" Christian asked.

"Yeah, you can go back to bed. I'm, uh, I'm just gonna finish up and go back to bed. Good night."

"Okay, good night, Willow," Christian said.

She heard the click of the lock as he left the room. Throwing the toothbrush under some running water, Willow planned her escape. Tired or not, she had to get home tonight.

When all was silent, Willow rose from bed. She sighed and glanced down at her clothes. She couldn't exactly put her dress back on. Never mind, she'd return the clothes later. As quiet as a mouse, she tiptoed to the doorway and listened carefully for any sound. Nothing. Pressing forward, she hurried down the creaky stairs. What was the time? The orange light from the stove glowed in the darkness. Just before midnight.

"Going somewhere?" a husky voice whispered.

Willow paused, a small gasp escaping her. Christian. Turning slowly, she looked up into his amused eyes. "I need to get home."

Christian came closer, invading her space. The smell of him filled her senses and the desire to be held by those strong arms and the security they promised scared the life out of her. A friendly half smile hung from his lips, a teasing light dancing in his eyes. Butterflies fluttered inside her. Goodness he was handsome.

"Do you want me to walk back with you?" His hand brushed against hers as he slid them into his front pockets. She shivered again.

"No, I'm okay. Thank you again for tonight." She ignored the longing she felt to stay right where she was and opened the door. A rush of cool night air filled the kitchen, slapping her back to her senses. She needed to get home and get away from Christian. "Good night." She stepped out onto the porch.

Christian's warm hand wrapped around her arm, drawing her back. "Will you be okay?"

She swallowed hard then impulsively kissed his cheek. "Thank you, Christian. I'll see you around." Then she hurried into the darkness, Christian's eyes burning into her back. She wouldn't look back, she wouldn't. Something had changed between her and Christian tonight and she wasn't ready to deal with it.

Felicia's house was silent now. Everyone was either passed out or had gone home. She tiptoed through the door. Stepping lightly over shapes strewn all over the dark living room, Willow searched for her shoes. Where were they? A shudder raced down her spine when her eye landed on Ethan's prone form beside the couch. Memories assaulted her, and her stomach lurched in protest. *Don't think about it, Willow.*

In a dark corner something sparkled, her shoes. Thank goodness. She hustled to the corner almost tripping over Brady, who lay in a drunken coma, half on and half off the stairs. Without thinking twice about it, she opened the front door and let herself out into the night air. Taking a deep breath and releasing it, she climbed into her car and drove away, glad to be going home.

Her house stood like a dark sentinel as she pulled up the drive. The T.V. was still on in the den. It covered the sound of the creaking door and her almost silent steps up the stairs. Her parents wouldn't notice how late she was or that she was wearing something completely different from what she left in. Heart racing, Willow closed her bedroom door and sank gratefully onto her bed. She'd made it. The movement sent up a puff of clean woodsy air. Christian. Lifting the t-shirt up to her nose, she inhaled, again amazed by the warmth and security the scent brought.

Annoyed, she threw herself down on her bed, her thoughts staggering through the events of that night. From entering the party, to Ethan, to being outside with Ethan, shivers racked her body again and she quickly focused her thoughts on Christian. Who was this boy who'd been so kind and considerate to her; despite the way she'd treated him the last few times they'd met?

What did he think of her? Did she care what he thought? Why did it matter?

Exhausted and confused by the sudden onslaught of emotions, Willow rolled over and pulled the blankets over her shoulders and closed her eyes. Surprisingly the one she dreamed about that night was not Ethan, but a boy with dark hair and the softest pair of brown eyes she'd ever seen.

"Willow, wake up."

Willow started awake, almost smacking her mother in the face in her rush to sit up. Adrenaline thundered in her veins.

"What, Mom?" she said and flopped back into her pillows, hand at the center of her chest.

Her mother looked slightly taken a back by her tone, but then that familiar expression of pained acceptance came again. "Felicia is waiting downstairs for you. I thought you were sleeping over at her house last night?" Her mother's words were stilted, and Willow knew she had better come up with a good explanation quickly.

"I decided to come home last night. I didn't feel like sleeping over. Felicia was busy when I left so I didn't get a chance to tell her." The lies slid out, leaving a sour taste in her mouth.

Her mother bought it. She *hmphed* and left the room. Thirty seconds later Felicia flew into the room.

"Willow, oh my goodness, where were you? I looked everywhere, and no one knew where you'd gone, who you were with. I thought maybe I should call the cops to search for your dead body."

Willow rolled her eyes. "Relax, Felicia. Take a load off." She tapped the rumpled cover beside her.

"What happened last night? Why did you leave?"

Willow tried to hide her shudder. She didn't want to tell Felicia about last night . . . she didn't want to relive what had almost happened with Ethan. She certainly didn't want to tell her about Christian. So, she lied, just like she had to her mother. "Nothing happened. I was tired."

Felicia frowned. "Are you sure you're okay?"

"I just need a shower and to wake up a bit more."

"My neighbor came over this morning—Christian. He wanted your number. Do you know why?"

Butterflies fluttered in her stomach, Oh Christian. "I don't know." She shrugged and tried to appear nonchalant. "I guess for the science project. Maybe he's too afraid to ask me for it himself." Another lie.

Felicia snorted. "Will, if there is one thing I know about Christian, it's that he's not afraid of anything. Maybe he likes you."

Willow burst out laughing. Felicia had to be crazy. Christian and her? What a nightmare. Felicia frowned and then shrugged.

"Oh Felicia, you've got to be kidding." She gasped for air. "Christian? Oh, Felicia you are insane."

"Whatever, Will. Are you gonna tell me what happened? I mean, Ethan looked so sad and lonely this morning. He didn't know where you'd gone either."

Willow felt sick. How dare Ethan even . . . "Turned out he's not my type." She pulled the sleeve of Christian's sweat shirt closer around her. His amazing smell surrounded her, bringing with it peace.

"Wait is that Christian's?" *Oh no.*

"No, of course not," she lied. *Please believe me.*

"Are you sure? I know he has one just like it."

"Just a coincidence. So, is Alex home this weekend?"

"Yeah, and he is in a mood. Brady and his bros left such a mess that Alex and I will probably be cleaning for the rest of the day." With a loud blast of music, Felicia's phone sprang to life. "Speak of the devil. I've gotta take this. I'll see you tomorrow."

"Thanks for checking on me."

"Sure. You may wanna check your phone." She tossed the pink device onto the bed beside Willow.

"Yeah." A minute later Felicia was on her way home, and Willow was alone with her thoughts.

The phone screen remained black as she pushed the power button. It needed charged. She plugged it in and waited a few minutes for the battery to fill enough for her to switch it on. There were six missed calls from Felicia, three from Amy, and two texts from Brad. Right at the top of the list was a missed call from an unknown number. She pushed the voicemail dial button, waiting in anticipation for the message. Secretly, she hoped it was from Christian.

"Hi, Willow, it's Christian. I just wanted to check if you are okay. I got your number from Felicia. I hope that's okay. Anyway, I hope you feel better. Bye."

The urge to cry almost overwhelmed her. With shaking hands, she added Christian to her contacts then pressed the little green button. She needed someone who knew about last night, someone who understood. And right now, the only person was Christian.

SIX

The irritating sound of the phone ringing forced him out of his Willow-centered thoughts. Sliding the phone open without seeing who was calling, he put the phone to his ear. "What, Jack?" he asked.

"C—Christian," came a hesitant voice.

Willow. Willow was calling him. Why was Willow calling him? Did it matter? She was calling him. "Sorry, hi, Willow. I thought you were Jack. Are you okay?" He forced out each word, his tongue tied in knots.

"Yes, I'm fine."

Again, an awkward silence rested between them.

Christian cleared his throat. "So, what are you doing today?" He braced himself for some snarky answer.

Instead, she said, "Nothing much. You?"

Who was this girl? He felt the urge to get to know her, and it scared him. Taking a deep bracing breath, he said, "Nothing much. Mom and Dad are at church. You want to do something?" The words left his mouth before he could censor them. An equally stunned silence answered him. *Bad move, Christian.* "Never mind. I'm sure you're busy with your friends and have better things to do."

"No, I mean, yeah, I'd like to do something with you. Coffee?"

Christian took the phone from his ear and stared at it. What the heck had just happened? Willow had agreed to go somewhere with him?

"Are you there?"

Christian rubbed the back of his neck with an agitated hand. "Yeah, Willow, I know a great place. I could—" Did he dare ask? "Can I come get you?"

Another pause, then, "In an hour?"

"That sounds great." Was this really happening?

Willow rattled off her address and ended the call. Christian stared at the phone in his hand, wondering if he was indeed in a second dimension. Willow Rysen had agreed to have coffee with him. He ran through the shower then hurried downstairs to grab some breakfast, narrowly missing a collision with his mother at the fridge. His parents were home early.

"Goodness, Christian!" His mother stepped back. "You're in a rush." She studied him, tapping her lower lip with her forefinger. "You look . . . "

Christian swallowed then managed to say, "I'm going out with Willow for coffee."

"The girl from last night?" Her surprise couldn't have been more evident.

"Yup."

"Be careful, son. That young girl is very troubled."

Christian nodded. "Perhaps she just needs to be shown how to be better."

His mom smiled. "Maybe. And you're the one to do it?"

"I don't know." He hugged her. "Thanks for caring, Mom."

A long driveway led up to Willow's house. It didn't take any stretch of the imagination to see Willow's family was loaded. He checked for the third time that he had the right address. Nerves buzzing, he parked beside a black, expensive looking car. It probably belonged to Willow's father. Her father, why hadn't he thought of that sooner? *This isn't a date, Christian,* he reminded himself. Was he really doing this? Taking a deep breath, he pulled his hands off the steering wheel and forced his feet out the car and up to the large house.

Bracing himself, he knocked. Instantly, the door swung open revealing a different looking Willow. He stared, stunned beyond words. Her hair hung loose around her shoulders, and she wore a blue top and dark wash jeans. She looked beautiful—a huge difference from the Willow he'd taken care of the night before.

"Are you ready?" he asked in a quiet voice.

"Yes," came the breathy reply.

Her hand trembled ever so slightly as she pushed a brown wave behind her ear. Christian watched her amazed, heartened by her obvious display of nerves. She'd always oozed confidence whereas he faked his most of the time, but today, they at least had one thing in common.

"Shall we?" He offered his elbow like an old gentleman.

Willow giggled. "Thank you."

Together they walked to the car, Willow's lavender scent lingering in his nose. Bringing them to stop beside the passenger door, Christian opened the door.

"My lady," he joked, gesturing to the door.

Willow didn't move.

"What?" he asked.

Willow smiled and slid into the car. "Nothing."

A horrible awkward silence descended as Christian started the car and pulled onto the main road. After several minutes, Christian stuffed away his shyness. "So, how're you feeling today?"

"Okay, I guess. I had a few nightmares but other than that . . . " She shrugged, a faint pink glowing in her cheeks.

His gaze involuntarily wandered over to her. Willow was relaxed and carefree. Her beauty lodged like a hard stone in his chest. What was he doing? Why had she agreed to meet him today? Did she have the same confusing emotions as he did toward her?

"Christian, if you keep staring at me, we're going to end up in a car accident." She didn't sound bothered by the fact. If he guessed right, she felt the exact opposite. And the smile on her lips . . .

He turned back to the road. "Sorry. Do you mind if we go to Anna's?"

Anna's was a beautiful coffee shop set in the forest outside of town. Since the weather was beginning to warm, Christian really didn't feel like being stuck in the mall today with the hundreds of people rushing around.

"That's fine." She paused, twirling her hair around her finger. "I wanted to thank you again for last night. I know you and I don't get along and never really have, but thank you for coming to save me last night. If you hadn't . . . " her voice trailed off.

He shuddered, it wasn't somewhere he wanted to go either. Christian reached over and took her hand into his. He didn't know where this sudden bravery came from, but he was sure it had something to do with Willow. He gently rubbed his fingers over her knuckles and gave her a reassuring smile. Willow smiled back and surprisingly didn't pull her hand away. With one last squeeze, Christian let go.

Shyness disappeared, and conversation flowed at an unhurried pace until they arrived at Anna's. Christian jumped out, swung around the car, and opened the door for Willow. She stepped out and shivered, her face pinched.

"Willow, before we go in there, can I ask you something?"

"Yes?"

"Why did you agree to come with me today?"

Willow flushed and muttered, "Well, uh, you did save me, and we need to discuss our project?"

As genuinely as the words were said, something in Christian's gut told him that they weren't true. There was something else going on here. The gentle mid-morning breeze ruffled Willow's dark hair, the sun light sending little sparks of light over it. Mesmerized, Christian sucked back his worries.

"Table for two, inside or outside?" The hostess asked.

Christian tilted his head toward Willow. She smiled slightly and shrugged.

"Outside please, Zoe," he said, taking the name off the girl's name tag.

Together, they followed Zoe to a booth outside in the lush garden. The sun shone between the dark green trees that lined the edge of a yard. Bright colored flowers of all kinds sat neatly potted along the walkways and tables. On impulse, Christian tugged a bright yellow flower out from one of the pots and tossed a coin into the jar. He handed it to Willow.

"For you."

Willow's cheeks flushed, something fascinating her about her shoes. "Thank you."

"Here you are. I'll be back in a moment with the menus." Zoe gestured to a wooden booth with red vinyl seats in the middle of the garden. The seats were canopied with a large, bright blue umbrella.

Christian and Willow took a seat opposite each other, lapsing into silence as they took in the vista around them.

"Do you come here often?" Willow asked.

Christian smirked. "You know that sounds like a bad pick up line, right?"

"What I meant was is this a place you go to regularly? I've lived in this town all my life and haven't been here. It's gorgeous."

Not just the garden was beautiful. "My mom loves this place. She used to bring me here a lot when I was a kid so that I could be more socialized."

Willow laughed. "I take it you're an only child?"

Christian nodded. "Mom has epilepsy. The doc told her that because of it and a hereditary heart condition, it would be dangerous for her to have any more. So yeah, it's just me. What about you?"

Willow shrugged. "I don't have any brothers or sisters either. I guess I was enough for my parents to handle. Sometimes, I wonder if my parents wanted kids." Her glum expression twisted his heart. At least he knew he was loved.

"You okay?" Christian asked. He waited for Willow to look up at him. When she lifted her head, a hint of some forgotten memory lingered in her blue eyes. "You can trust me, Willow," he murmured.

Willow sat up straight, leaning her back against the red cushion, the sadness in her eyes disappearing like yesterday's news. "Last night was pretty wild." A frown marred her pretty forehead. Her eyes welled, and she blinked quickly.

"Not quite the word I would use," Christian said, not sure where this conversation was going. When Willow didn't carry on talking, Christian knew that there was more to her statement than she was letting him know. "So, the science project?"

Willow's grateful smile stole his breath.

"Are you guys ready to order?" Zoe asked.

"Ah yeah, I think so. Willow?"

"Sure, what do you recommend?" she asked him.

"Well, everything here is great. Though one of my favorites are the breakfast pancakes."

"That sounds good. I'd like to order that and a Diet Coke."

"No coffee?" he teased.

"I think I'll take up tea." They laughed, both privy to the private joke.

"I'll have the same with a coffee milkshake instead of the diet soda please."

"Sure. Is that all for you and your lady?"

"Uh, we're not, uh . . . " Warmth flooded Christian's neck.

"We're just science partners," Willow said, her cheeks tinged red.

"Sure, I'll be right back with your order."

"Thank you, Zoe."

Zoe returned a few minutes later with their stacks of pancakes.

"What side do you want?" Willow asked, pouring more syrup on her pancakes.

Christian shrugged. "The Christian side, I guess. My parents are believers."

"Makes sense."

"I take it yours aren't?"

Willow shrugged. "God isn't a good word in our house."

They lapsed into silence and enjoyed their food. Every now and then, Christian would look up, amazed that Willow was opposite him. They talked about normal things, nothing tense, just everyday conversation. Today had turned out to be very strange day.

"Why?" Willow placed her knife and fork in the center of the plate and pushed her plate back. She took a deep swallow from her drink.

"Why what?" he asked.

"Why don't you believe?"

Christian scratched his head, although his mother spoke to him regularly about God, he'd never had someone ask him so directly. "I don't know. I mean, my parents say that God is in control of all things and everything happens for a reason, but I'm not so sure. If God was in control, then couldn't He have given my mom another baby? Don't get me wrong, I know my parents love me." He trailed off. For some reason, he wanted her to. "My mom used to cry at night, begging God for another child." The memories of those nights sometimes haunted him. He'd never told his parents about them and he was sure he never would. Rubbing a hand down his face, Christian glanced up at Willow. Why was he telling her this? Why did she even care? And, yet something compelled him to answer her. To confront his own reasoning.

He swallowed hard as Willow's face softened. An expression he'd never seen grace her face astounded him. It was almost like she cared.

Clearing his throat again to release the wad of emotion there, he took a long swallow of his milkshake then asked, "Are you ready to go?"

Willow drank the rest of her soda and gathered her things. "Yeah. I'm ready."

Conversation was stilted on the way home. Christian was sad that their time together was coming to an end, but a bad feeling settled into his stomach as he dropped Willow off at her house and climbed back into car.

"Stop borrowing trouble, Christian," he whispered.

SEVEN

Monday morning, Christian shouldered open the door of the school. Willow's disdainful gaze met his, and a heavy wave of unease settled in his gut. He should've known. Meek and gentle Willow was all for show. He was such a fool.

Willow turned to Felicia and whispered something, Felicia said something in response, and they both giggled. The kind eyes from yesterday had been replaced by a hostile, hateful scowl. This was who Willow really was.

"Dude," Jack walked over to him, "what the heck happened here?" He gestured to the hallway littered with bodies. Girls huddled together with tear-streaked faces, some brave enough to toss hateful glares over in Willow and Felicia's direction.

"This is my fault." Christian fisted his hands into his pockets.

Jack stared back perplexed. "Your fault? How is anything Willow Rysen does your fault?"

Christian was oddly pleased that Jack had seemed to overcome his fascination with Willow. "You remember the party at Felicia's house on the weekend?

"Yeah, sure. The one that busted up our game."

"Well, Willow was attacked. I rescued her from a guy, my mom and I patched her up, and she left sometime after that. I took Willow to Anna's yesterday."

Jack's eyes grew wider with each word Christian said. "You and Willow went on a date?" Jack's deep voice rose in disbelief.

"It wasn't like that. I think she agreed because she thought she owed me."

"That sounds about right. But I still don't see how you taking Willow out makes this," he swept his hand out toward the teary-eyed girls, "your fault."

Christian sighed. "Come on, Jack, don't you see? Willow felt vulnerable with me. Me—the very kind of person she despises came to her rescue."

Understanding slowly spread across Jack's face. "Man, I'm sorry."

"So much for being the good guy, huh?"

"Tell me about it." Something painful lingered in Jack's eyes. "But now what?"

"Now, I handle this." Swallowing down his disappointment, Christian stormed over to Willow and Felicia. "You know, Willow, you need to go home, think about everything you are, then change it because you aren't winning any friends here." He came to a stop a foot away from her, punctuating each word.

Willow's face turned to stone, her eyes spitting sparks, but Christian didn't care. It was obvious to anyone that his previous encounter with Willow had been nothing more to her than a way to pass the time.

A wave of "No ways" echoed down the hallway. A flock of Willow followers surrounded them. Christian didn't care, it was now or never.

"Who do you think you are?" Felicia shoved Christian's shoulder.

"Someone who is sick of your queen and band of harpies."

"How dare you."

Brad took a step toward Christian. Jack did the same, flanking him. The two of them glared at each other in challenge.

"Really, Felicia? I've known you since we were kids, and I didn't think you'd sink to this level. Was Trent not good enough for you anymore?" The words poured out of Christian before he had time to censor them.

Hurt flickered in Felicia's gaze at the mention of Jack's older brother. A wave of haunted crimson filled her cheeks, quick glances passing between her and Willow.

Remorse twisted Christian's heart at the look of betrayal in Felicia's face and the faint flush in Willow's. There was obviously some history there. Squeezing the bridge of his nose, he took a deep breath and let it out. This wasn't him, and this wasn't his problem after all.

"I'm sorry," he said. The words barely squeezed past the concrete that had taken residence in his throat. He grabbed Jack by the shoulder and pulled him down the hall to their first class. This day had started out far worse than he'd hoped it would.

The lunch bell rang, and Christian sighed. Finally, he could spend some time not thinking of Willow and all the things that had happened this morning. The hallway bustled with students as he made his way out of his government class in search of Jack.

"So, how did things go with you and Ethan?" Felicia asked.

Christian paused and honed in on the voice that answered.

"Oh, you know . . . " A little giggle that sounded all too forced to Christian followed the words. "We had a lot of fun together. He was a bit rough though." Willow sounded proud of the fact.

"Oh, I bet you did." Amy joined in the giggles of the other girls.

Christian stalked around the corner and fixed his gaze onto Willow. He raised an eyebrow in challenge. Just a little rough?

"Yeah, I was really d . . . " Willow's eyes went wide and a blush seeped into her cheeks. Without a word, she pushed past him and stormed off to the lunchroom.

A strong but small hand gripped his arm. "I don't know what you think you know, but you made a very big mistake taking her on. Believe me." Felicia growled. Then she and the rest of Willow's entourage smirked at him and chased after their queen, giggling all the way.

Christian hoped he hadn't just made the worst mistake of his life. Before today, he'd known Willow was not to be messed with, but it looked like he was about to experience her wrath firsthand.

The quick tap of her heeled pumps distracted Willow momentarily from the sea of raging anger within her. Just who did Christian think he was speaking to her like that? She was Willow Rysen for goodness sake, and she didn't take shade from anyone. A wicked smile lifted her lips. If Christian wanted to be a hero, she'd make sure he'd have someone to champion. Feeling more settled than she had in days, she wandered off to her next class. Paulette, Christian's cousin, would be the perfect target.

The waxing moon gave the night an inky darkness. The perfect cover for her revenge on Christian and his Goody Two-shoes friends.

Felicia and Willow giggled and pointed from their position behind the shrubs that made a wall around Paulette's house.

"This is going to be the best prank ever," Felicia shrieked beside her.

Willow shushed her with her hand. They moved toward the house, trying to stifle their snickers with their hands and more or less succeeding. Felicia handed her a pack of toilet paper rolls and took two cans of shaving cream out of her backpack, shaking them as they crept closer to the house. Willow stopped underneath a huge, green tree that looked like a Christmas tree and began to rip the plastic off the toilet rolls. She looked up to see Felicia inching her way closer to a blue car parked in Paulette's driveway. Shaving cream cans ready in hand.

One by one the toilet rolls sailed into the air and landed with soft thuds on the surrounding trees. "Willow," Felicia whisper shouted, "Run!"

Somewhere in the house a light turned on and Willow ran.

"Get in!" Felicia shrieked again.

Willow dove into the car just before Felicia slammed her foot down on the gas and they were out of there. "That was great," she said laughing until her sides hurt. Felicia laughed and laughed until the tears ran down her face. She high-fived Willow. "Did you spray the car?" Willow asked., gasping for air.

"Yup, every last inch of it. Let's see how she likes that."

They pulled into Felicia's driveway. Willow noticed a shadowy figure on the front porch next door. Even without seeing his face, Willow knew it was Christian. Shame filled her so quickly that she almost choked on it.

"Will, are you okay?" Felicia asked, her huge smile fading.

Willow nodded and tried to smile back. "I'm not feeling well. I think I need to go home."

Felicia frowned and looked in the same direction Willow had just been looking. "Is he the reason you don't feel well?"

Willow froze then vigorously shook her head. "No, what do you mean?"

Felicia watched her for few moments, "Are you sure? You've been acting so weird when he's around." She couldn't know, could she?

"It's nothing. He's just my science partner."

Felicia whistled through her teeth. "The science partner who took you on in front of the whole school. And makes you jump every time you see him. Honestly, Will, I think there is more to this than just a science partner. You're not crushing on Christian are you?"

"What, no! I can't stand him." Her stomach twisted in knots at the lie. The truth was that seeing Christian threw her for a loop. Somehow in the last week, his opinion of her started to matter.

"If you say so," Felicia didn't believe her. Maybe her lie was not as convincing as she'd hoped.

They climbed out of the car. Willow deliberately kept her back to Christian's porch. She didn't want to see his cold look even though the hairs on her neck told her he was watching her every move. Waving goodbye to Felicia, she climbed into her own car and drove away, swearing she would get over her ridiculous fascination with Christian Blythe.

In the days that followed, Willow went out of her way to avoid Christian. If he approached her, she turned in the other direction. If he called, she ignored it.

However, late at night when the house was dark and quiet, the nightmares would come and then so would Christian. Each time she closed her eyes, he would save her. Swooping in at the moment she most desperately needed him as if in relentless pursuit. Right before Ethan could . . . Her eyes flashed open and she bolted up in her bed. Sweat covered her body, her breath coming out in thick gasps. She was safe, in her room. Ethan couldn't hurt her.

Christian's comforting words rang in her ears. "I'm here Willow. You're safe."

Flopping back down onto her soaked sheets, she counted her breaths and focused her mind's eye on Christian as her heart rate gradually slowed. Feeling much calmer, she pushed herself up and off her bed, taking the steps two at a time. Maybe some water or possibly warm milk would help her fall asleep again.

The glow of the kitchen light shone brightly in the dark night. A shadow moved within its depths. Willow peeked around the corner. Her mom sat at the island, her shoulders hunched. Willow could tell from the slight sounds she made and the minute movement of her shoulders that she was crying.

"Mom?" Willow stepped into the room.

Her mother's back stiffened and she hastily wiped her eyes. "Willow, what are you doing up?"

"Couldn't sleep. I thought maybe some milk would help."

"Yes, that might help. Good night, Willow," her mother whispered. She pushed her chair back, picking up something from under her hands and slipping it into the folds of her robe.

Another crack appeared in Willow's walls. She took a step forward before stopping herself. What was the matter with her mom? Why had she been sitting alone in the middle of the night weeping? She struggled to remember the last time she'd actually had a decent conversation with her mother and came with nothing. And it bugged her. Her hands still shook but they were steadier than when she'd woken. She poured herself a glass of milk and slurped it down. Then she walked back to her room hoping that now she might get some much-needed sleep.

EIGHT

Frustration boiled through Christian as he stalked down to the football field. His anger raged to new heights at Willow and her band of followers and their overwhelming sense of superiority over the other students in Bethel. Especially those students who worked hard and did more than sitting on their butts and scraping through their classes. Paulette's teary face was clear in his thoughts. She'd called him this morning before school, sobbing quietly over the mess left in her garden. Clenching his jaw, he forced himself to calm down. He still couldn't understand why Willow's brush off still made him so angry. He just wanted to be rid of her presence in his dreams at night.

Willow ran down the bleachers and launched herself at one of the football players. He caught her then set her on the ground, and she tossed her hair and laughed. Christian scowled. This shouldn't bother him so much. After all, Willow was just being Willow. Scrubbing his hand through his hair, he took a deep breath. He had been looking for Willow for a reason after all. He walked up to her, took her by the arm, and led her further down the field. Far enough away that their discussion could not be heard.

"What do you think you're doing?" Willow whined, anxiously glancing between Christian and her friends.

"Don't worry, Willow, you won't die if they see you with me," he said dryly. "They know we're science partners don't they?"

Willow stilled her anxious prancing and scowled. "Of course, they wouldn't think we are anything else now would they?" Willow's face flushed. She crossed her arms over her skimpy top, her glare mutinous.

"So, it's gonna be like that is it? That's real mature." Christian snorted.

The bristling anger surrounding Willow dissipated. "What do you want?" Suddenly, the girl from the weekend was looking back at him. It was amazing what that one soft statement did to cool his rabid temper.

"Why Paulette?"

Willow flushed. "I don't owe you an explanation for my action."

"No, you don't, but honestly, my cousin. What did she ever do to you?"

"Nothing, everything. She's just like you. Judgy and smart and—" Willow stopped and pressed her lips together. She shook her head her, eyes conflicted.

Christian sighed. "Are you still coming tomorrow?"

Willow shrugged. "I don't really have a choice, do I?" Her words lacked the spiteful heat from earlier.

Chuckling, he said, "No, not really."

Willow smiled back, then her eyes went wide. The disdainful expression she'd been wearing all week settled on her face again.

"Are you done here, Will?" Felicia asked, coming up behind him.

Christian tensed. He could almost feel the burn of the acid in her words. He glanced one more time at Willow. "I'll see you tomorrow." He hoped that her expression would change, but all she did was nod, her fleeting smile long gone. Christian's heart sank. A fool's hope. He drove home, counting the hours until Willow Rysen would no longer be a part of his life.

Hands on her hips and eyebrows raised, Felicia glared at Willow. "Nothing's going on right?"

Willow snorted. "Are you nuts? What I'd like to know is how you seem to know him so well. He knows an awful lot about you and Trent."

A dark red river spilled into Felicia's cheeks. "He's best friends with Jack, Trent's brother." They stared at each other, each remembering a painful memory on a night so long ago. Hurt pinched Felicia's mouth. She sidestepped Willow and followed the other girls back to the locker room.

Willow's gaze trailed over to the empty school parking lot where Christian's car had been earlier. He didn't know what it was like being her. The expectations, the unwritten rules, and the distorted loyalties. This was all she'd ever known.

But Christian made her feel things she'd never felt, never expected to feel. And if she was completely honest, feelings she didn't want to feel. Stuffing her emotions back into the abyss, Willow wandered to her car, flicking her gaze to the locker room now and then. The football players and the girls spilled out into the weak afternoon sun. They laughed and flirted, not a care in the world, and for the first time, she didn't feel like joining them. Maybe she would go to the mall. Spending Daddy's money always made her feel better.

The car took a direction of its own as she drove. Instead of the mall, she pulled to a stop in front of Anna's coffee and cake shop. She had no idea why she was here, but there was something about this place that gave her a measure of peace.

"Can I get you something, honey?" a sweet-faced elderly lady asked her. She reminded Willow of her grandmother—the only one who'd ever seen her. Just Willow.

"Is it okay if I just wander around the gardens for a bit?" she asked.

"Something troubling you?" the lady asked.

Willow paused, a burden heavy on her shoulders. "I don't know." It was the most honest answer she'd given in a very long time.

"I'm Vera." Vera took Willow's hand between hers and led her to one of the tables off to the side of the shop.

"I'm Willow."

Vera sat her down then took a place opposite her. Willow didn't know what to say. Her insides felt like they were pulling apart. Vera reached over and took Willow's hand, bringing her attention to her. Her hand was soft and aged like Grandma Jean's had been.

"Honey, I don't know what troubles you, but I've been on this earth for over seventy years, and I can tell you there is only One that can help a troubled heart."

Willow went rigid. "How do you know that?"

Vera smiled softly. "Jesus told me."

"I don't know about Jesus, but I'm sure you're wrong. Religion isn't for me."

Vera *tsked* under her breath. "I wasn't talking about religion. I was talking about Jesus. I'm not here to 'shove Him down your throat' like you young people say, but I felt like I needed to tell you that Jesus is the cure for a troubled heart. Take your worries to Him. He'll listen." Vera stood up and smiled. "Would you like some apple pie?"

"Thank you, I'd like that. I'm just going to . . . " Willow tilted her head toward the open garden behind her.

Vera smiled again. "You do that. I'll be right back."

The gardens smelled like fresh happiness, and her fingers trailed softly over the pink, blue, and violet petals. There was something about the scent of tulips, bluebells, and hyacinths that pulled her back in time.

The names of the flowers came flowing back to Willow as if her grandmother was walking beside her pointing to them. Her gran had been an avid gardener and loved the outdoors. She'd shown Willow how to garden every chance she got. Funny that Willow hadn't thought about her gran in years. When she'd passed, Willow had shoved away the memories and pressed into the wild side of high school life. Oh, how she missed Grandma Jean.

Vera motioned Willow back over to a table and set a plate of steaming apple pie in front of her.

"Here you go, deary. Warm and sweet. You enjoy that now."

"Thank you." Willow sat down and inhaled the scent of fresh apple pie.

Vera went to attend on a small group of elderly ladies that had taken residence at the booth where she and Christian had sat. Willow frowned. There was something about that boy that made her insides feel funny. She sighed and dove into her dessert. The apple pie was warm, the mixture of cinnamon, apples, and brown sugar teasing her taste buds and pressing her further into her memories of Grandma Jean.

"Always remember, Willow. God and prayer are two of the most important things in life."

NINE

People smiled and laughed, old friends greeted each other, and new friends were being made. Hallelujah Gospel Church was bursting at the seams. Obviously, Pastor George was someone many people wanted to hear speak.

Christian looked around for Willow and spotted her standing alone at one of the entrances, her expression masked. His heart jumped, then a second later, wariness settled in him as he remembered the cold shoulder he'd been given all week. Exhaling loudly, he walked over to her.

A look of relief swept her features when she focused on him. He stumbled over his feet. She was actually happy to see him?

Willow smirked, then her expression changed back to the one of haughty indifference he hated.

"Hi." He came to a halt beside her.

"Hi," she said, her eyes guarded.

"I see some seats over here." He gently took her elbow and led her over to their seats. Sparks and tingles skated up from her into his fingers.

"Is your mom here?" Willow asked as she walked beside him down the aisle.

"Yeah, they are over on the other side with Paulette's parents."

66

Silence hung awkwardly between them as they found their seats. Willow tugged her arm free and sat down. Disappointed, Christian sat down, preparing for an evening filled with conflict.

Willow sank down beside him. "I have better things to do on a Saturday night than be in a church," she muttered. Her voice harsh but raw.

"Oh, like last week . . . " He froze. Guilt seeped into him at the unabashed horror on Willow's face. Christian rubbed the back of his neck. That was uncalled for no matter how much he felt she deserved it. "I'm sorry." Regret cut his voice.

Willow sat stock still beside him. Slowly and carefully, he reached over and took her cold hand into his, waiting until she turned to face him. Fear swirled in the depths of her blue eyes.

"I'm sorry. I wish . . . How are you after last week?"

"I still have nightmares but you . . . " Her words trailed off, her expression indecisive. Then it shifted into something that looked almost like resolve. "I have nightmares, but you always come. You always save me before they get too bad." Her shoulders hunched defensively.

A bizarre happiness snuck into his heart, and it bounced wildly in his chest. Had she just . . . did she . . . what was this?

Christian swallowed. Words failed him, and his emotions mixed up. Pushing past the events of the week he said, "I'm glad you're okay. Willow, I—"

Gently extracting her hand from his with a small smile, she stopped him, "Thank you for being my hero, Christian. Let's just leave it at that." Willow sat back in her seat, appearing absorbed by the stage at the front of the room. Every now and then her eyes would flick to him.

Did he chance his heart again, knowing that this could blow up in his face spectacularly? To heck with caution, he licked his lips. "Can we meet at Anna's tomorrow to compare notes?"

"Maybe we should just concentrate on the stage." Willow didn't bother to glance at him.

"I'll buy you apple pie?"

Willow smirked.

"Okay, final offer. We go to Anna's to compare notes, and I buy you apple pie and a Diet Coke."

"I'd like that," she whispered. A soft smile bloomed on Willow's lips.

Music filled the auditorium. Something restless inside him settled. She'd said yes to his crazy question. Perhaps there was hope after all.

A new Christian band came onto the stage and sang a few songs. The tension from the past week lifted from his shoulders, releasing him from its heavy weight. His spirit soared, the music drawing him into the songs and the lyrics and melodies filling his heart. The words of the final song spoke to the empty, dark places inside him. It pulled at his heart, silently answering the questions that so often held him back. The song reached a crescendo.

Come home and live in My love. Here you will find answers, here you'll find peace. Come home.

A new, complete knowledge settled in Christian, a surety, a peace. The music ended, and he sat down, his heart open and listening.

"And now, we'd like to welcome Pastor George onto the stage," the band leader said before ushering his mates off the stage.

Christian lifted his eyes to the stage, expecting to see some stuffy old guy in a suit and tie. Much to his surprise, a young man in a green sweater, jeans, and sneakers walked onto stage. He looked to be in his thirties and carried a small black book in his hands.

"All heaven declares the glory of the Lord." He pointed to the little black book in his hand. "It says so right here in Psalms 19:1, yet scientists around the world believe that Christianity and science cannot agree. They say that one is a work of fiction and the other a work of fact. However, if I looked at the sky today and said the sky was blue and you said the sky was pink. How could either of us be proven wrong? We could maybe find a third person and let them give their opinion on the color of the sky, but we would just be hearing someone else's opinion. How would we know without a doubt the sky is blue? We could go into all kinds of theories and hypotheses about the color, but even these theories are based on human theory, which is fallible."

The man took a drink of water from a nearby stand before continuing. "Take how scientists see the Bible. They believe that the Bible is a book written in ancient times by a bunch of people who have nothing in common. The result is then a bunch of stories written that either bring people comfort or condemn them to hell. But what if I told you that I could prove that the Bible is the living breathing word of God and one-hundred percent true and accurate? Do I have your attention now?"

Pastor George smiled as some of the people in the audience laughed. Christian could see the twinkle in Pastor George's eye.

"In Genesis 1:1 it clearly states, 'In the beginning, God created the heavens and the earth.' Yet some scientists still believe in the big bang theory." He clapped his hands together. "Poof." He clapped loudly again. "And the universe." The audience laughed, but Pastor George didn't skip a beat. "This theory is directly contradictory to their ultimate theoretical scientific theorem—every action has an equal and opposite reaction; cause and effect; and therefore, where input is needed to create output. The universe is governed by laws. Laws carefully planned and put into place by God Himself, the Intelligent Designer. Laws such as these could not have been implemented or would not work if two mere somethings struck each other in random occurrences in the depths of space. There had to be an input for the universe to be an output. And yes, that input is God. His words speaking into the output that is the universe. Thus, proving the scientific theory, input is needed to create output."

Pastor George went on to discuss other examples of science and the Bible agreeing, quoting various verses to prove the fact. He spoke of the various tests done on the Bible, and the historical parallels between it and secular history.

"All that being said, let's get down to what's really important. Who of you here has ever heard of man named Jesus? A man Who loved each and everyone one of us here so much that He died on a cross to save us from our sin? A man Who died and was raised by God on the third day and now lives in eternity?"

Many people in the audience raised their hands. Christian sat forward in his chair and he saw Willow do the same.

"The Bible is the story of Jesus. Throughout all of history, His story has been told and is still being told. God's love for us is so great, His mercy so unfathomable, that through Jesus's death and resurrection we can have eternal life. If we would just believe."

Christian finally understood what his mother had been talking about. A fuse from deep inside him lit up and seamlessly sewed together all his doubts, filling each spot inside him with the knowledge that God loved him. He knew he'd done nothing to deserve that love, but despite his running and pushing God away, God loved him and wanted to have a relationship with him. Something he didn't know he'd been searching for his whole life suddenly arrived and reached out to him. Conviction fell. Christian crashed to his knees, feeling the love and mercy of God on his bowed head.

"If tonight's message has spoken to you and you would like to invite Jesus into your heart, then I'd like you to say a prayer with me." Pastor George said. "Dear Lord Jesus, I give you my life. Come into my heart and make me whole. Please forgive me for my sin and make me clean. I want to live my life for You from this day forward. In Jesus's name. Amen."

The last words left Christian's mouth, and a gush of tears of gratitude streamed down his face. Love and peace filled him. He stayed kneeling and silently prayed, "Heavenly Father, I'm sorry. I know that You are all-powerful, and although I don't understand why You didn't give my mom another child, I know that You knew it was for the best. I'm sorry for setting You aside all the time and listening with half an ear when Mom and Dad spoke of Your love and mercy. Thank You for chasing after me. Thank You that You love me so much despite all the times I've run and done things my way. Help me to trust in Your leading for every day. Please help me live for You. Amen."

Eventually, the tears stopped, the weight of the past being washed away with them. He ran a shaky hand over his cheeks, mopping up the stream of liquid drying there and pulled himself up to sit in his seat again.

The rush of joy he felt, he wanted so badly to share. When he glanced to the seat next to him, he found it empty. Willow was gone.

God be with her, he prayed, worry clenching his stomach. He hoped Willow would find her own way to Jesus just like Christian had.

"Christian, are you okay?" His mother's soft hand rubbed his shoulder. "Is it Willow?"

Christian chuckled. Even Willow couldn't mar this beautiful moment. "No," he said, "these are tears of joy, Mom. I understand what you've been trying to tell me all these years. I finally understand."

His mom pulled him into a tight embrace. "Oh, my boy. Thank you, Jesus. Thank you, Jesus!" She repeated the words over and over again and tears freely fell down her cheeks.

His father joined the embrace, gathering both against his burly chest. Christian had never seen his father cry, but tonight, heavy droplets glistened in his brown eyes. He kissed Christian's mom on the cheek then clasped Christian's shoulder. "Tonight, our boy has come home." Christian's face ached from smiling, but there was nothing he could do to make it stop. His joy was so complete, so full. Smiling felt like the least he could do.

When his mother pulled back, she looked around him. "Where did Willow run off to?"

"I don't know." His worry intensified. Where had she gone?

TEN

Adrenaline pumping, Willow ran. She had get out of here. But the heavy foyer doors refused to budge.

A man in a blue suit walked toward her, his expression concerned. "Are you okay?"

Willow glanced at him. His eyes were brown, just like Christian's. She gritted her teeth, a knot forming in her throat. She couldn't breath. Desperation pressed her forward. Willow pulled the doors, silently thanking her lucky stars that the door gave way.

The foyer was empty. Willow's eyes welled. She so desperately wanted what Pastor George's words promised. So desperately wanted to be accepted for just her, not for what she wore, or the boys she kissed, or how much she drank. Grandma Jean's smiling face swam in her mind.

She wouldn't cry here. She had to leave, had to get away from the voice urging her to turn around and accept what had been so freely given, so lovingly offered. To accept Jesus as Lord of her life.

The blistering cold of the night rolled onto her skin, and she let out an involuntary gasp. She'd forgotten her coat. Tipping her head back and taking in a deep inhale, Willow gazed at the stars above her. Pastor George's words persistently circulated in her mind, the truth of them staring back at her in the golden blazing dots and the dark, midnight blue sky.

She wanted to believe, but what would Felicia think? Her parents? Her dad hated anything linked to God. She shivered again and walked over to her car. God wouldn't want her anyway. God was for nice people like Christian.

Willow took a deep breath and locked her emotions away. She forced a smile. Her friends wanted her. With them, there was nothing to be ashamed of, no guilt to feel. Swiping her finger across the screen of her phone, she dialed Felicia's number.

She cleared all emotion from her throat. "Hey, where you at?"

Felicia paused then asked, "Will, are you okay?"

"Fine, fine. Where are you?"

"We're at Amy's house. I thought you had that church thing tonight?"

Willow wiped her eyes again, her voice steadier. "The guy was finished talking, and I skipped out on the music. I'll see you in a bit."

"Cool, see ya," Felicia said and ended the call.

Keeping her mind deliberately blank, Willow drove. When her phone rang a few minutes later, she ignored it. Felicia knew she was on her way and the only other person who would call tonight was the very person that she couldn't speak to.

After parking her car outside Amy's house, Willow checked her raccoon eyes in the mirror and quickly cleaned up her makeup. Her clothes would have to do, although normally she wouldn't arrive dead at a party like this.

A nervous butterfly danced in her stomach, but she pushed her way into Amy's house. Laughter and the deep throb of rock music crashed over her. The usual party scene surrounded her. Felicia and Amy stuck funnels into Brady and Jace's mouths, forcing white liquid down their throat. Her resolve shifted, and she felt her eyes fill again. *Get it together, Willow.*

She needed something to drink. As she headed for the kitchen, she paused, shook her head, and continued on to the fridge. She grabbed a bottle of clear liquid and looked at the label. One drink wouldn't be so bad.

She downed the contents in one go. The alcohol tingled through her. After grabbing another bottle, she sashayed out of the kitchen and into the living room, swinging her hips to the relentless beat. The alcohol and music wiped away all thought of tonight's events just as she'd hoped it would. This was easy, familiar.

"Hey, Will." Brad stepped by her and tentatively took her hand in his.

Willow smiled and giggled. "Hey you."

"Want to dance?"

"Sure, why not."

Brad lowered his mouth to hers. Willow closed her eyes and tried to kiss him back, but all she could see was Christian. No, don't think of him. He would only ruin what little composure she still held. Alcohol burned down her throat again, fuzzing her thinking and she pressed closer to Brad.

Brad trailed kisses down her neck. "I missed you, Will," he said in the deep, husky voice she'd enjoyed all too often. Giving over to the feeling again, she kissed him.

The music and the alcohol did what she'd come to do. Forget.

A few hours later music still pumping in her blood, she stumbled out of Amy's house, laughing hysterically as she fell against the hood of her car. Her hands trembled on her key fob, and for some reason, that was hysterical, too. She slid behind the wheel and giggled again as the engine roared to life.

Her phone pinged in her pocket. She reached down to get it, accidentally hitting the brake pedal. Her car lurched, and the phone slipped out of her hand and under her seat. She reached down to retrieve it, gaze shifting from the road into the dark recesses at the bottom of her car. Where was that thing now?

Look up! a voice roared in her head. Willow sat up in time to see her car hit the guardrail. In an act of pure instinct, Willow braced her arms against the steering wheel, adrenaline pumping her fuzzy thoughts crystal clear. Her headlights faded into the inky blackness that pooled off the side of the cliff.

Willow screamed.

She was going to die tonight.

Christian's face and Pastor George's words converged in her mind as Willow stared down the barrel of her fate. Her car slowly tipped forward toward the waiting maw of night and balanced precariously over the edge of the mountain.

She shouldn't have gone to that party tonight. She should have told Christian that he was special to her. There were so many things she should have or shouldn't have done.

The voice came again: *It's not your time.* And with a great thud, she was neatly back on the road.

Blood pounded through her arteries in a desperate race. Her breath hitched in her chest and tremors consumed her. What had just happened to her? She rested her head on the steering wheel, taking a few deep breaths and thanking whoever was out there in the universe that she wasn't dead.

It seemed like an eternity that she sat there breathing and staring into the darkness as if it held the answers to her bizarre night. Her limbs felt heavy, her mind distant, and she was so very tired. She climbed out of the car, walking slowly to the large dent the guardrail had formed in her front bumper. For the most part, her car was unarmed. Climbing back into the car, she turned the ignition over a few times. Finally, the car started again. There was only one person that could help her find out what had happened tonight. If he would talk to her.

Willow drove to Christian's house and climbed out of her car, deliberately skulking in the shadows so that no one from next door could see her. The cold night seeped into her thin clothes, and she shivered. She had no idea which room was his and knocking on the door didn't seem like a good idea. She'd probably run into his mom again.

Rubbing heat into her arms, Willow walked slowly around the house, stumbling over dips and rises in the lawn hidden by the darkness. A light came on in one of the rooms upstairs. Willow stopped, making sure the darkness covered her. The window opened, and she could see Christian, his face troubled, staring at the house next door, his expression sad and wistful.

"Christian?"

ELEVEN

Christian started and leaned further out the window. "Willow? What are you doing here?"

Her chestnut hair danced wildly in the wind around her, her eyes puffy and red. There was a small cut over her right eye, and a trail of blood ran from her left eyebrow down the side of her face.

"Can I please talk to you?" she asked.

"I'll come get you at the backdoor," Christian said, reaching for his shirt.

Christian hurried down to the back door. As soon as he opened it, Willow ran like a wobbling rocket at him and threw her arms around his waist. Christian stumbled backward then cautiously folded his arms around her.

"What are you doing here?"

Willow took a deep breath then dissolved into tears. "Oh, Christian, I'm sorry. I don't know . . . " The rest of her words were muffled against his chest.

"Come inside. It's freezing out here." He curled his arm around her lower back and led her into the warmth of the house. Not wanting to disturb his parents, he maneuvered her to the den and onto the sofa. "Willow, it's the middle of the night. Where have you been and why do you smell like a brewery?"

Willow bowed her head and fidgeted with her hands in her lap. "Uh . . . I . . . "

"What happened? Please tell me."

Willow sniffed again. Her eyes searched his for something, then she reached over and took his hands. A sad smile lit her features, her fingers moving gentle patterns over his knuckles. His heart stuttered and stumbled, growing more confused the longer they sat in silence.

Finally, Willow said, "I know I shouldn't be here, and I'm probably the last person you want to see." Christian made a negative sound. Willow pressed a firm finger against his lips. "You're the only one who could possibly tell me what happened."

"Tell you about what?" Christian stared down at her, confused by the emotion that shone in her eyes.

Willow trembled, a new set of tears falling down her alabaster cheeks. "I'm sorry. I didn't know where else to go."

"What have you gotten yourself into?"

Willow shook her head and took a few more deep breaths. "I don't—it's all kind of blurry."

"Just tell me what you remember."

The frown deepened on Willow's forehead. "I was driving home from Amy's party. The next thing I knew, my car was hanging over the edge of the cliff off Old Miner's ridge. Something strong and powerful shoved my car back, and I heard a voice telling me that it wasn't my time." Willow sucked in a deep breath and looked up at him. Her eyes glistened in the pale light of the den.

Christian leaned back in his chair. Overwhelming fear hammered through him, although he didn't let it show. She'd almost died tonight.

"So, what do you think?" Willow shifted again, her blue eyes meeting his, her hands tightening around his.

"About?"

"About the car accident, and I don't know, me almost meeting my end at the bottom of the cliff. I feel like I'm going crazy."

Christian took a deep breath. "Willow, God saved your life tonight."

Willow's eyes didn't harden into the icy blocks he'd seen so often. Instead, they welled with tears. Wonder filled her expression, then a deep, unstoppable sadness washed over it. "God wouldn't do that for someone like me. Not for someone who's done the things I've done." Willow withdrew her hands from his and stood.

Christian stood with her. "God loves you enough to save you. You heard what Pastor George said tonight. Jesus loved us so much that He died on the cross for us. God sent Jesus to that cross for us, Willow. For people like me and people like you. To God, we are all precious and loved equally."

Denial flashed in her eyes, and she shook her head. Her big blue eyes looked into his then down at her hands again. Without preamble, she launched herself toward him and wrapped her arms around his middle.

Christian forced himself to stay still. He cared about Willow. Not in the way that one friend said to another, but in the way that would end in nothing but trouble. He cleared his throat and said, "How about I go get some water for you and you go to the bathroom and clean up?"

"What?"

Christian gently touched the bump above her eye. His fingers tingled at the contact with her soft skin.

Willow winced. "Right."

Christian led her to the bathroom and flicked on the light. "There are towels and stuff in there. Use whatever you need. I'll be right back."

Willow stood in the center of the room for a moment then whispered, "Thank you, Christian."

Christian nodded and ran his hand through his hair to settle his wayward emotions. He had half a mind to kick Willow out and send her home, but the other half, the crazy half, cared whether she made it home in one piece or not.

His mom stood in the kitchen, her back against the counter behind her and a cup of tea in her hands. "What are you doing up?"

"Willow's here. Down in den. She's had a pretty rough night."

His mother's eyes went wide. "Is she okay?"

"A little banged up but seems to be okay. She's in the bathroom cleaning up."

"Why is she here?"

"I don't know. She says something happened and thinks I'm the one to explain it to her."

"Is she drunk again?" His mother sounded worried. Christian could understand. Willow had a reputation after all.

"She smells like it, but her voice isn't slurred or anything."

"Are you okay to talk to her? Do you need me to help?"

"No, I'll just see what she says, make sure she has water, and send her home. You go on back to bed."

His mom reached out and kissed his cheek. "I'll pray for you. Maybe take her some coffee."

Christian nodded and prepared a cup of strong, black coffee. Then, grabbing the cup of coffee with one hand and a water bottle with the other, he walked back toward the den.

"Christian?" his mom called.

"Yeah?"

"Be careful."

Christian grinned—his mom knew him too well. "I will. Love you, Mom."

The light from the bathroom shone brightly, Willow's movement forming shadows across the open doorway. He placed the coffee and water on the table next to the couch and sank down onto the sofa.

Willow stepped out of the bathroom and shifted nervously in front of the doorway. "Okay, I'm done."

"Come sit down," Christian said, shifting to the far side of the sofa.

Willow took the seat right beside him, the warmth of her body and her clean scent filling his nose. He shifted again, but he was already at the end of the sofa and couldn't go anywhere else.

Willow seemed oblivious to his movements. She reached for the mug of coffee. "Is this for me?"

"Yeah, ah, strong black coffee and water."

Willow lifted the coffee. She took a tentative sip and grimaced. "Is there sugar in this?"

Christian smiled slightly and shook his head. "Just drink it."

After taking three big swallows of the warm coffee, Willow placed it back onto the table and grabbed the bottle of water.

"Christian, I—" Her words faded and she stood. "Thank you for tonight. I should probably go." The bottle shifted between her nervous fingers.

Christian rose and slid his hands into his pockets to keep from reaching for her. "Sure, anytime."

He followed her out of the den and to the front door. She pushed it open but hung back. A force he couldn't control drew him to her. He wrapped his arms around her waist and tugged her toward him. Willow sank into the embrace.

As if time stood still, he brushed his lips softly against hers branding their feel into his memory.

Willow stiffened and pulled away. She stepped through the open door. "I'll see you around." Then she climbed into her car and disappeared into the darkness.

Christian leaned against the doorframe, cold seeping slowly into his bones. What had just happened?

TWELVE

Sunday morning brought a beautiful sunrise and a new day. Willow smiled and stretched her arms above her head. She couldn't remember the last time she'd sleep so well. Her thoughts lingered on Christian, her smile turning down. She would never forgive herself if she did anything more to hurt him. But she could dream what it would be like to be someone special to a boy like Christian.

An urgency she couldn't explain pushed her from her thoughts and bed. She dressed quickly before hurrying downstairs to grab a quick breakfast. Her mom and dad were in their usual places on a Sunday morning, side by side, coffee cups in hand, reading the morning paper. She used to think it was cute that they did that, and she found that she still did. Where did all this sentimentality come from?

"You're up early," her mom said, surprise coloring her tone. Her gaze slowly trailed down Willow's body.

Willow shifted under her scrutiny, butterflies dancing in her stomach.

"Are you going somewhere?"

"Just out for a bit." She hoped her mom wouldn't see what a mess she was. It seemed that crying had become her new favorite past time, and she'd had a hard time hiding the puffiness of her eyes with makeup.

Her mother nodded and returned her attention to the paper. Her dad didn't even look up.

Breakfast bar in hand, Willow raced out the door, her heart thumping with nerves. Opening the GPS app on her phone, she set it for Hallelujah Gospel Church.

The parking lot was filled. After parking near the entrance for easy exit, she braced her dancing nerves and headed to the church.

"Hello, dear, is this your first time here?" A kind lady asked as she walked through the door.

Her face felt stiff and she tried to arrange a smile on it. "No, I was here last night to hear Pastor George speak." Her voice sounded breathless even to her ears.

The woman smiled back. "What a lovely message don't you think? I hope you enjoy today's service." She handed Willow a folded paper and ushered her into the church auditorium.

The familiar feeling of terror filled her. Who was she kidding? What was a girl like her doing in a place like this? The urge to run tugged at her, but her heart told her that she needed to be here. Pushing down the urge to flee, Willow settled into a seat.

The band took the stage, followed by the choir, and lively music filled the room. Willow wasn't a fan of singing; she hadn't sung anything in her life worth mentioning, but she found her voice lifting with the others around her. A warm, loving presence enfolded her; and in that moment, she knew God loved her. Despite her wretchedness, He loved her.

The tears that had gathered earlier spilled out, first in ones and twos then in torrents. She closed her eyes and asked God's forgiveness for every selfish, nasty, unthoughtful, prideful thing she'd ever done. Repentance for the parties, the drunkenness, and the reckless lifestyle fell from her lips. The wall around her heart disappeared, and a new, softer heart took its place.

She felt vulnerable and scared yet so loved and full. A peace she'd never knew existed settled into her, and for the first time in a long time, she felt hope. Hope that she could be loved just the way she was. With a slow crescendo, the singing came to an end. Willow wiped her tears. Her knees gave way beneath her and she landed with a thud back in her seat.

Pastor George walked to pulpit. He took a hold of the same little black book that he'd used last night and held it up, pages open. "Today's key passage is taken from Matthew 10:32, 'Whoever acknowledges me before others, I will also acknowledge before my Father in heaven.' What does this mean for Christians today? Are we called to apologize for our faith, hiding behind principalities and societal niceties? No, we as Christian are called to live with distinction for our Lord and Savior Jesus Christ. The same can be said on a more personal level as well. Is there something that you hide in the secret places of your office, your house, or maybe your heart? Things that you know are wrong, but you do anyway, hoping that if you ask forgiveness for the sin often enough God will just forget about it?" Pastor George scanned the crowd.

"There are two wolves inside a person. A black one that is filled with every deplorable thing a human being can do, every sick sin that can be carried out by a human's nature, and then there is the white wolf that is filled with everything that is given to and expected of us when we give our lives to Christ—hope, faith, compassion, and kindness."

Willow leaned forward in her seat, her heartbeat hard in her chest.

"The black and white wolves are constantly in combat inside each Christian. The wolf that you feed is the wolf that will live within you. If you choose to keep sinning, your sin will consume you. If you give your life to Jesus and live for Him, you will have eternity. Which wolf will you choose to feed?"

When the sermon ended, Willow strolled back to her car and couldn't find words to express her feelings. Her heart was at peace, she was loved, and she was forgiven. Her gaze flitted around the packed church parking lot and landed on a familiar set of chinos and dark hair. Her heart leaped in her chest. She cared about him as more than a friend. Maybe some day she'd have the courage to tell him what had happened to her.

Thank You, Jesus, she whispered and climbed into her car.

The house was silent except for the faint buzz of the lawn mower from the back yard. Her mother was probably out there alongside her father pruning for the spring. Ignoring the urge to join them, she hurried up to her room.

Her room had always been a kind of a haven for her. A place to hide her secrets, a place to keep her secrets. Her parents seldom wandered in. They'd learned the hard way that her space was private. She cringed, remembering the words that had passed between them and her about her attitude, her lifestyle, and her friends. Words that had cut her deep and words she'd said that cut just as deep.

She swallowed back the tears of regret gathered. How could she fix that? Her phone beeped for what seemed to be the twentieth time since she'd walked through the door. Ruffling through her bag, she pulled it out and settled onto her couch beside her bed. Notifications on her social media exploded like little drops of rain all over her screen. Great. Her usual urge to immerse herself into the drama of the weekend overpowered her and she settled in to catch up. After all, Felicia would ask on Monday. When all the messages had been read, Willow wandered around her room, restless. Maybe she should just go ahead and do her homework. A smile lifted the side of her lips, homework reminded her of Christian. Science it was.

"Willow, lunch," her mother called a few hours later.

Willow quickly checked her face and settled it into a blank mask. She loved her parents, but the decision she'd made today would not be easy to explain to them. A feeling of foreboding flashed inside her. What would her parents think of her new view on life? She could guess, and it wouldn't be pretty. Right now, she didn't have the strength or information to stand up to their opinions.

"Do you mind if I stay in my room to eat?" She stepped into the kitchen.

Surprise flickered in her mother's eyes, but she handed Willow a plate. "Yes."

Willow smiled. "Thanks, Mom."

The astonishment in her mother's face made Willow feel awful. There was a lot to fix here. Maybe Susan would be able to tell her how.

THIRTEEN

Willow pulled another outfit from the closet then threw it back in. Surely she had something that didn't show quite so much skin. She was going to be late for school if she didn't hurry. She grabbed a pair of long dark wash jeans—they were tight but not indecent—and a midnight blue sweater from the back of her closet. A light application of makeup and a clip in her long hair, and she was as ready as she'd ever be to face her day.

"Is everything all right, Willow?" Her mother glanced over her for the third time during breakfast.

"Yeah, why do you ask?"

"Did you do something different with your hair?"

"Just the same old, same old." Willow took the last two bites of her cereal and scooped up her bag and keys.

She felt different, and judging by the way her mom hadn't complained about her outfit or lack thereof, she looked different. Willow was sure her mom thought she'd packed a different set of clothes in her bag to change into at school. She'd done it before. There were many times she'd lied to her mother about where she was or what she was doing after school or what went on at parties. A new emotion that felt like shame squeezed her lungs. She hadn't even told them what had happened at Felicia's party all those weeks ago. Resolving to tell her mom the truth from now on, she arrived at school.

She sat in her car for a long time, thoughts of Christian circling in her mind. She knew he was something special to her, but she didn't for a second believe that he would feel the same or that anything would come of her obvious infatuation with him. She was too messed up, and even though God had forgiven her, she didn't think that Christian would if he knew even half of what she'd done. Pushing aside her black thoughts, she climbed out of the car. It was now or never.

"Willow?" Felicia made a beeline for her from the entrance of the school. Her eyes went wide, and a disgusted sneer lifted her lips. "What is that?" She gestured to Willow's outfit.

Willow quickly glanced down at her outfit knowing that her and Felicia's clothing choices were as opposite as day and night. Their motto was "Nothing is too short or too tight." At least, that's what hers used to be.

Felicia raised an eyebrow. "Your mom giving you a hard time about your clothes again?"

Willow could have lied and blamed it on her mom, and everything in her wanted to, but a small nudge in her heart told her to tell the truth. "Nah, I decided to dress a little differently today."

Felicia shrugged, her expression confused. "Whatever." Hooking her arm into Willow's, she dragged them both into the school building.

Willow blew out a relieved breath. Maybe today wouldn't be so bad.

"Oh joy. Nerd boy alert." Malice dripped from each of Felicia's words.

Willow swung her gaze around and spotted Christian. She wanted to say something, was ready to say something. Anything. Christian was so much more than just his brains.

Christian blushed and turned away. How could he not have heard Felicia's words? They were said so loud the entire student population of Bethel heard.

"Come on." Willow dragged Felicia to their first class. Looking back over her shoulder once or twice to . . .

"What are you looking at?" Felicia asked.

"Nothing," she muttered and slipped into her desk.

"Hey, Will, check out Bailey." Felicia leaned across her desk and pointed to a girl two desks in front on them. Willow lifted her eyes, dreading what she knew was coming. "Hey, Bailey, I don't think that dress agrees with your body type." Felicia spat out.

Amy and the others laughed. Willow plastered a fake smile on her face, her gut churning.

"All right, class, your attention please," Mrs. Mars, the English teacher, chimed.

Felicia leaned over again, ignoring the teacher's words. "So, what happened to you this weekend?"

Willow's stomach dipped, a lie on the tip of her tongue.

"Ms. Wren, you will see me after the lesson," Mrs. Mars said, saving Willow from answering.

"Why?" Felicia said.

A rush of red slowly climbed into Mrs. Mars neck, although her voice stayed calm and forceful. "To discuss your inability to keep quiet when asked."

Felicia faced burned, and her eyes flashed angrily. "Who does she think she is?" she muttered under her breath.

Willow sighed and touched Felicia's arm. "Just leave it. Save yourself the aggravation you know it's going to cause when you get a trip to Principal Rory."

The shock at Willow's response couldn't have been clearer on Felicia's face. "Who are you and what have you done with Willow?"

Willow shrugged, shifting uncomfortably in her chair. "Maybe we should just get to work." Willow turned her attention to Mrs. Mars. This was so much harder than she'd thought it would be.

The library was unusually quiet when Christian walked in for his second period science class. Jack followed him in on his way to meet his partner at the computer terminals to collect some research they'd done the day before. Christian and Willow had been assigned to the library today to get some work done, although he wasn't sure that his mind was with him enough to do more than stare at her. When he'd seen Willow walk in that morning, the difference between her and Felicia glaringly obvious. He'd had to brace his feet to stop them from walking over to her to see if she was okay. The Willow from Saturday night was there in plain color.

"Hey, bro, you with me?" Jack asked.

Tearing his gaze from Willow, he turned to Jack. "Yeah, I, uh . . . " he cleared his throat. "Never mind. You were saying?"

"I asked you if you were up for a game this afternoon?"

"Yeah, yeah, sure," he said, although he was so distracted Jack might have asked him for the moon.

Jack laughed and looked in the direction Christian had been staring. "Something you want to tell me about you and that one?" Jack gestured to the girls, their backs facing them as they talked and giggled in a huddle

"Jack, this may come as a huge surprise to you but . . . " Christian scrubbed his face. "I like her."

"Which one?"

"Willow," he sighed. How to explain.

Jack's eyebrows shot up and he stopped. "When? How?"

Christian quickly explained all that had happened in the past few days.

Jack blew out a low whistle between his teeth. "Man, that is. Wow. So, you and her?"

Christian nodded and rubbed the back of his neck. "Yeah, I guess. I mean, I kissed her. What's going on with me? This is Willow Rysen."

"She doesn't sound like Willow." Jack slapped a heavy hand on Christian's shoulder. "I mean coming to you for help? Hanging out with you? That sounds really strange." Jack suddenly laughed. "So, how was it?"

"How was what?"

"The kiss, man! How was it?"

"Uh, well she didn't run away screaming, so I guess it was okay." Christian could feel the stain of heat moving into his cheeks.

Jack grinned then laughed again. "So, you and Willow?"

"Willow doesn't date nerds."

"But she also doesn't kiss them. That should mean something, right?"

Did it? Christian wondered. He cared about Willow, and he couldn't stop dreaming about her. But they didn't stand a chance.

Willow turned into the room, her expression happy but cautious.

Christian waved to Jack, moving toward her. "There's a table in the back we can use." He shifted his laptop to his other hand, almost dropping his books in the effort. Snatching them up just in time, he cleared his throat, his neck heating.

"Okay." Willow covered a small smile with her hand.

Willow followed Christian into the back of the library. His heart raced inside his chest, his palms sweaty. Why was he so nervous? They sat down at the table, each laying their books aside, although neither of them reached out to them to begin working.

"How are you?" he asked.

"I'm good. And you?"

"The same."

Silence descended again. He looked over at Willow's bowed head, her gaze fixed on the table. What was happening here?

"Willow about Saturday . . . " His words trailed off as Willow shifted, threading her fingers through each other. Slowly, hesitantly, he reached over and laid his hand over her tangled hands.

Willow stilled, her bright blue eyes flicking up toward his. Something swirled in them. But what was it? Did it have a name? His left hand followed his right and gently untangled Willow's fingers and rested them in his. Sparks lit between them, running from her hands to his.

"Saturday?" Willow whispered.

"Regrets?" Christian asked. He wasn't really sure what he expected from her.

Willow slowly shook her head. "No."

Christian had to strain forward to hear the words, not sure he'd heard them correctly.

Taking her hands from his, Willow flipped open her laptop. "About the project."

"Willow," Christian said.

"The point Pastor George made about creation was very interesting. Especially when he quoted Genesis 1:1."

"Willow," he said again.

"And about each action having an equal and opposite reaction."

"Willow!" His voice came out louder than intended, but it had the desired effect.

Willow stopped, her stunned expression staring back at him.

"Willow, what now?" Christian whispered. He wasn't sure he wanted an answer, but he had to ask.

Willow's expression grew sad. "Can we please concentrate on the project?" Her voice was pleading, and her eyes held an unmistakable longing, a wish. A small indication that gave Christian hope.

Give her time, the words whispered into his inner depths in a voice that sounded oddly like his mother's. Taking a deep breath, Christian conceded. Willow was scared—that much was obvious.

"So, what did you think about his point on the accuracy of the Bible?" He opened his laptop and turned it on.

Willow smiled gratefully then shuffled through a large pile of notes. "Well, give me a second, I know I did do that point."

Christian's eyes widened. "You did the homework?"

Willow looked back at him, a slight red tinge in her cheeks. "Ah yes, you know, product of a slow social life."

Laughter bubbled out of them. They both knew that wasn't true.

"You want to tell me about it?" Christian asked, secretly please he'd made her smile.

"Let's just say that I had some time on my hands Sunday. Ah, here it is." She handed a handwritten paper to him.

"Okay. Are you really okay after Saturday?"

"Yeah, I think I'm okay." A mysterious light shone in her eyes, making everything about her beauty that much more blinding.

Christian blinked and shook his head as if coming out of a dream.

"Check this out. I found this verse that talks about the water cycle. It proves that science and the Bible agree about how vapor returns to the clouds and then comes down as rain. It's Ecclesiastes 11:3. 'If clouds are full of water, they pour rain on the earth. Whether a tree falls to the south or to the north, in the place where it falls, there it will lie.'"

"Wow, that's great, Willow." The red flush in her cheeks endured her to him even more.

"Thanks. It's been a weekend of discovery for me." Willow shrugged.

"That slow social life again?" Christian teased.

The red in Willow's cheeks brightened and Christian felt a shift in his heart. What was it about this Willow?

For the remainder of the lesson they compared notes. Each time their gazes met, he felt himself fall a little further. And for the first time, the end of the lesson came too soon.

Christian reached over to grab his notes, his hand accidentally brushing against Willow's. Willow stopped him and wrapped her shaking hand around his for second before letting go. That small gesture made the drop of hope he'd felt earlier expand till it took over his heart.

"See you tomorrow?" Willow asked.

Christian smiled and nodded. "Tomorrow."

FOURTEEN

Smiling at her unplanned boldness with Christian, Willow walked into the lunchroom and plunked down beside Felicia.

"Where did you disappear to on Saturday night? I thought you were going to sleep over?" Felicia punched her fruit salad with her fork.

Willow blushed and poked at her own salad. "I, uh, decided to go home. I wanted to sleep in my own bed."

Felicia frowned, her eyes forming slits. "What is it you're not telling me?"

And there it was. "Can we talk about this some other time, please? Did Alex come for the weekend after all?"

Felicia nodded. "Yeah, he did." The topic changed from Alex to Saturday night again. Felicia told them about her experiences at Amy's party, followed quickly by the other girls.

The more they spoke, the harder it became for Willow to hide her disgust and shame. *Is this what every Monday had sounded like before?* Nausea roiled in her gut, and she swallowed hard.

"Excuse me, I need to, uh, I need to go to the bathroom." She gathered up her stuff and rushed out, holding her hand over her mouth to keep the contents of her stomach down. Sliding the lock on the cubicle, she sank down onto the closed toilet and took deep, gasping breaths. In through her nose and out through her mouth, in through her nose and out through her mouth.

She stared in abject horror at her hands, remembering when her voice had joined in with the stories. Lies and half-truths woven together to make a better story. Her face burned. Was this her? Was this what she wanted? If she told her friends what had happened this weekend, she was sure they would shun her. She would lose them, her status, everything. Was she really considering this? Giving up everything for Jesus? And Christian? Where did he fit in?

She pushed out of the bathroom stall and over to the sink. She stared at herself in the mirror and watched as the stony, fake mask she'd always worn slid over her features. Settling around her eyes and mouth like an old friend. A sardonic smile lifted the corner of the mouth in the mirror. She could always fake it.

And for the rest of the day she did.

"Denise, what lovely shoes. Did the charity store have a sale?"

On and on the insults and giggles went. Willow's face hurt with forced and deliberate laughter, and sometimes the words stuck in her throat before she pushed them out. The crushed expressions on her victims' faces pushed at the gate where she kept her guilt locked behind.

"Willow?" someone called from down the hall.

She closed her eyes. She knew that voice anywhere.

"Willow, are you okay?" Her shoulder tingled as his warm hand enfolded it.

Steeling her features into an indifferent mask, she turned to face him. "What do you think you're doing?"

Christian took a shocked step back, the light of concern in his eyes replaced by a hard look of hurt. "She's back then," he whispered. A sad smiled lifted the corner of his mouth, then he turned and walked away, not looking back once.

The rest of the week, Willow hid behind her mask, and each day the weight in her chest grew heavier and heavier. She could barely stand to look at herself in the mirror, a relentless battle raging between her conscience and her need to keep her friends. Pastor George's message about the two wolves repeated in her mind. The wolf you feed is the one that is the strongest. Willow knew which wolf she'd been feeding all week, and her chest ached.

"So, I'm planning a party Saturday night," Amy said over lunch on Friday.

"I'm in," Willow said without thinking. And the black wolf roared in triumph.

On Friday, Willow ambled into the science class bowed under the pressure of her decisions. Her gaze met Christian's. They'd been avoiding each other for the better part of the week. When given time to finish the project, she leaped at the chance.

"Mrs. Wilson." She raised her hand.

"Yes, Willow, what can I do for you?"

"May Christian and I please go to the library to finish our project? We have some stuff to discuss."

Mrs. Wilson's eyebrows rose into her hairline, and she motioned to Christian. "Sure, Christian, you may go with her."

Wariness settled over Christian's features, but he picked up his stuff and followed her out of the room.

Willow's heart pounded relentlessly as she walked to the library, knowing that Christian was behind her. Could he hear it?

"I can do this, I can do this," she muttered to herself. She had to get through this project then get away from Christian as fast as she could.

The library was cold, and a few lights shone in its dark interior, giving it a gloomy and depressed feel. Willow shivered and walked over to the science section. She placed her books on the wooden table and faced Christian, keeping her face downcast on its glossy surface. Her resolve wavered. She squeezed her fingers together then wiped her hands on her jeans. She hoped Christian didn't notice how badly they shook. "We need to discuss our project," she began. "Here is my side of the argument, now you can do yours. As we agreed, I did the side that didn't agree that science and the Bible were compatible."

Thanks to a few sleepless nights that were fraught with dreams about Christian, her homework was done. The paper rattled softly as she pushed it over the table to him before sinking down in her chair.

"Willow," Christian murmured.

Willow lifted her head, giving in to her selfish need to see him. Her gaze collided with his and sent her heart into a frantic spiral that said only one thing. He did care. Christian's hand lay on the table, the paper resting near it. Willow fought everything in her not to reach out and touch it. To feel the warmth and security she knew was there. She swallowed hard, pushing down her emotions. She didn't know how much longer she could hold back the tide that pressed against barricade which held them there.

"Now you can get the grade you want," she said in fake cheerful voice.

Christian's shoulders sank. "Is that what you think? That this has all been about a grade?"

Surprise shook Willow's core. "It wasn't?"

"Maybe at first," he admitted, "but after that time we spent together, it wasn't only about a grade to me."

The wall around Willow's heart splintered, love gushing out, filling her, consuming her. Droplets formed in her eyes. He did feel something for her after all.

She pushed herself to her feet. "I'm sorry. I can't."

"Willow, wait." Christian's hand landed on her arm, his voice close to her ears.

She desperately wanted to turn and throw herself into his arms, but she couldn't. Pulling her arm free, she picked up her bag and rushed out the doors. The last thing she heard was a broken whisper of her name. Willow ran, the bathroom once again becoming her haven as tears trailed down her face. She couldn't give in and let him know how much she loved him.

No one could know.

Christian stared at Willow's retreating form. A science project? Did she honestly believe that was all there was to it? Okay, he hadn't given her any reason to think otherwise, although he thought he had through his actions. There had been an emotion lingering in her eyes, something that told him that she was hiding. Hurt transformed into understanding. Pushing aside his pain and confusion, he stood up and gathered his school stuff. He sent up a silent prayer, "Dear, Lord, please help Willow. Help her to see You. Help her to know that the life You promise her is worth it. I can see she's confused, so please help her to find You. Amen."

Feeling calmer and more at peace than he had all week, Christian went to his next class. It was up to God now and all he could do was wait.

FIFTEEN

The heavy bass coming from Amy's house pounded against the headache behind Willow's eyes. What was she doing? How she wished . . . She stopped that train of thought before it completed.

"Let's do this," she muttered. She plastered her fake smile on her face, smeared on a last layer of red lipstick to complement her smoky eyes, and adjusted her dress, pulling it up higher on her chest. Why had she let Felicia talk her into wearing this one tonight? Thankfully, it at least hung down to her mid-calf, so she didn't feel quite so naked, but the neckline was a lot lower than she felt comfortable with. A few weeks ago, she would have pulled it lower, but now, it felt wrong.

She climbed out of the car and slammed the door shut with unnecessary force behind her. Arranging her mask again, she sashayed into the house, running her fingers flirtatiously along the cheek of some cute boy at the door. His eyes glazed over, and a breathy laugh that turned her stomach escaped her.

The air stank with the smell of alcohol, sweat, and depravity. Drunk kids fell over each other and did things she knew they would never do in the light of day. Despite the tepid air, she shivered and wiped her wet hands down her thighs, once again wishing that she'd listened to the voice inside her that had told her not to come.

"Willow." Felicia stumbled toward her and took a long swallow from the bottle in her hand.

One of the football players grabbed Felicia and forcefully pressed his lips to Felicia's, his arm bound around her lower hips. His hands eagerly ran over Felicia's body, and Willow's stomach turned.

"Drinks are in the usual place," Felicia said, coming up for air. Then she ran her hands up the boy's chest and pulled him close again.

Willow turned and walked into the kitchen before her breakfast made a reappearance. She opened the chest near the basement, taking one bottle out at time and sliding it back into the cooler. None of them held any appeal. Maybe she could find some pop somewhere. What was she doing here?

A pair of hands settled possessively on her hips, drawing her close to a hard, sweaty body. She turned, ready to slap whoever had dared to touch her.

"Hi, sweetheart. Remember me?" Ethan's fetid breath made her already unsettled stomach lurch. He leaned forward as if to kiss her.

Willow pushed frantically against his chest. "Let me go, Ethan."

"Don't be like that, sweetheart. We had so much fun the last time." The depths of his dark eyes turned hard with malice and danger. He pressed a hard kiss to her mouth.

Fear roared up Willow's spine, and she pushed Ethan back. *Oh no.* She glanced quickly around. Where was Christian when she needed him? *Right where you left him,* a voice sneered in her mind.

Felicia giggled and lost herself again in the football player. Amy was indecently spread on the sofa with another. Everyone around her seemed to having a wonderful time and took no notice of her and Ethan.

Ethan tightened his hold on her. "You want something to drink?" He raised the bottle in his hand to his lips and then forced it onto hers. "There's a good girl. Drink up."

Willow snatched the bottle from Ethan's hands. "I can get my own drink." *Oh God help me!* she prayed.

"Hey, Willow," Jace said behind her, his gaze hard on Felicia.

Ethan's death grip on her eased. Now was her chance. Willow thrust down on the hands bound to her hips. Ethan's grip broke and Willow ran for the door. She was in her car and on her way home before anyone could reach her.

Breaths still gasping out of her, Willow made a decision. She was done. She would embrace the life God had for her whatever it cost.

Willow's phone buzzed in her pocket, and she answered the call.

"Hey, girlfriend, where have you been?" Felicia's voice rang out.

"Uh, I went to ch—church this morning," Willow stuttered, her voice sounding weak in her ears.

Felicia giggled. "For your project again? Or was it for that boy?"

Willow shook her head even though Felicia couldn't see. "No, because I wanted to."

Felicia fell silent.

Willow sighed. "Felicia, it's not for me anymore."

"Will, are you okay? What are you saying?"

"I still want to be friends with you. I mean, we've known each other since kindergarten, but I don't want the parties and boys and alcohol anymore. I've changed."

"Is this because of Christian?"

"No, Felicia, I've made a decision to follow God with my whole heart." She paused then finally admitted to herself and to her friend, "And Christian. I like him. I mean really like him."

The line went dead. Willow sighed. That was the end of that then.

Once she arrived home, Willow marched into her room and to her closet. If she was going to change for the good, it was time to let go of the old Willow and embrace the new one. Ruffling through her closet, she pulled out all the clothes that shouldn't be in a teenage girl's closet and tossed them in a trash bag. Then she took out the huge black box she kept tucked in the back and shifted through the contents.

Sitting on top was a picture of her, Felicia, and Amy.

She frowned, remembering the fight she'd had with her mother over her bikini just before leaving.

"That bathing suit is indecent," her mother had said, and now, Willow couldn't agree more.

Shame filled her, and she wiped at the tears on her cheeks. She would have to leave her friends and their ways if she wanted to be different.

"Willow?"

Willow looked up. Her mother's concerned eyes grew larger and larger when she spotted the carnage around Willow's closet.

"Are you spring cleaning?" her mother asked, her tone ripe with curiosity. She eyed the bottles and paraphernalia lying around and a frown marred her features.

"Yeah, it's time."

No words passed between them as Willow walked over to her mom and hugged her tight.

Her mother's hands trembled as they rubbed Willow's back. "Are you all right?"

"I'm sorry, Mom, for a lot of things." She pulled back so she could look up at her mom.

"What do you want, Willow?" Her mother's features hardened.

Willow blinked hard and pulled her mom close again. "Nothing." The old Willow had always given affection for something in return. But she wasn't the old Willow anymore.

"Mom, can we talk?"

Her mother nodded, stunned again. Another tear trickle down Willow's cheek. She had so much to make up for. She took her mom's hand in hers and gently pulled her over to her bed.

"Mom, something happened last weekend, something wonderful. I gave my heart to Jesus, and I just wanted to say that I'm sorry. I'm sorry for all the times I've lied to you, shouted at you, given you attitude, and been disrespectful. I want to change, and I want to be better, a better daughter to you and Dad. I love you guys, and I know I haven't said it enough."

"Willow . . . " Her mother's words trailed off, and tears streamed down her soft cheeks. "Oh, my girl." She slid her arm around Willow's shoulder and pulled her into a firm embrace. For a long moment, they wept together, clearing away years of hurt and pain.

Willow wiped her eyes and pulled out of the embrace. "Would you like to come to the mall with me? Help me find a new, decent wardrobe?"

"Are you sure?" her mother whispered.

The old Willow never asked her mom for anything. "It would mean a lot to me."

"Let me fix my makeup and then we can go."

Willow waited in the front room for her mom to get ready, slowly mulling over all the events of the day. As she turned around, her mom entered room carrying a flat box in her hands.

"Willow, I have something to show you." Her mother held out the box. "I have prayed many nights that one day I would be able to give this to you. That one day I would see my daughter share my faith."

Unfolding the cover of the box, Willow lifted out a green and white leather-bound book. The Bible. Inside was an inscription with today's date. "Oh Mom, this is beautiful. Thank you!" Willow set the Bible back in the box and enveloped her mother in another hug.

"When we get back, I'll show you some of my favorite verses," her mom murmured in her hair. "Now let's go to the mall."

Smiling through her tears, Willow nodded. Finally, one area of her life was how it should be.

SIXTEEN

Christian did a double take as he entered the school building. A girl that looked remarkably like Willow shifted uncomfortably beside her locker. Her jeans looked new and fitted well, her peasant blouse was attractive but not revealing, and her makeup was soft and light. Her lips moved silently as she repeated something. His heart pitter-pattered as he walked toward her.

"Willow?"

Willow turned to him and pushed her dark hair behind one shoulder, getting it stuck between the strap of her backpack. He'd thought about her often over the weekend. What had she been doing at church?

"Hi, Christian." Her voice was quiet, unsure, and her gaze nervously jumped up and down the hallway before settling on her feet. To their left, he could see Felicia and her friends standing in a thick knot, whispering and staring in her direction.

"Is everything okay?"

"Much better now, thank you." She gently laid her hand on his forearm. The noise around them ceased as they fell into each other's gazes.

Christian tried to understand the message Willow was sending, hardly believing that what he was seeing could be possible. "Good. Are you ready to go to class?"

"Yes." She reached out and threaded her fingers between his. "This okay?" she whispered.

Christian nodded, the connection between their hands rendering him speechless. What had happened to Willow over the weekend?

Every eye followed them as they walked hand in hand to their seats at the back of the class. Christian expected her to pull her hand out of his and make some joke, but Willow stayed glued to his side.

The bell rang and Christian sat in his seat beside Willow, unable to tear his gaze away from her. There was something in her expression that made him think of a wary warrior finally at peace. Every now and then, she would shuffle through her papers, quietly repeating words to herself again.

Christian leaned over and gently tapped his finger on her notes. "You ready?"

Willow smiled. "Yes, I hope so. My heart feels like it is going to jump out of my chest right now."

"I know what you mean. I usually hate speeches."

Willow simply nodded. For a moment, silence hung between them. Willow opened her mouth a few times but no words came out.

"Willow, can I ask you something?" His heart banged against his rib cage.

Willow slowly nodded. "Okay."

"Why where you at church yesterday? I saw you at the end of the service."

A red flush filled Willow's cheeks. "I, uh, felt I needed to be there." She smiled again, the light of peace shining in her eyes.

Christian stared. He couldn't help it. This Willow who was at peace with herself was more attractive than any other girl he'd ever seen. Clearing his throat, he rested back into his chair while he put his notes in order on top of his desk.

"Okay, class," Mrs. Wilson began, "today is the due date for your assignment, and I'm sure you are eager to present your findings to the class. First, we will be hearing from Christian and Willow. Come on up you two."

Together, they stood and walked to the podiums set up before the class.

Christian set his papers on the podium and faced his classmates. He wanted to talk to Willow more, but this was important. He felt like he needed to convince Willow of what he was saying. "Mrs. Wilson, Willow, and my fellow classmates, science and the Bible were never meant to be seen as opposites. In Genesis 1:1, the Bible states that God created the Earth. Evolution postulates that creation was a result of the big bang—two rocks randomly clashing together to form livable conditions and intelligent life—life that evolved over millions of years from a single cell organism to a human man as a result of natural selection. However, the Bible clearly states that the Earth and man were created by an Intelligent Designer, God.

"Intelligent design suggests that complex life could not have occurred by a random act of natural selection. For example, take the Earth's position in relation to the sun. If the Earth was even a few more degrees closer to the sun, it would be too hot for life to exist; however, if the Earth was a few degrees further away from its current position, it would be too cold for life to exist. Therefore, a higher being, God, must have placed Earth in the perfect position between the sun and other planets so that life could exist.

"Also, there are many instances where the Bible told the truth before science came to recognize it as truth. For example, it was once believed that the Earth was flat. Nowadays, science has proven with the use of telescopes and satellites that the Earth is round. In Isaiah 40:22a it says, 'He sits enthroned above the circle of the earth.' The Bible had it right from the first. The second example is that centuries ago it was believed that light didn't move and had no properties. This has since been disproved by science. Anyone ever heard the phrase, 'as fast as the speed of light?'" People around the class chuckled. Christian smiled and looked over at Willow, she was smiling back.

"But again, the Bible always had it right. In Job 38:19a it says, 'What is the way to the abode of light? And where does darkness reside?' showing that light does have property and movement. These and many examples once again prove that although atheists, evolutionists, and most scientists would like to believe that the Bible and science are on opposite ends of the intellectual scale, they do in fact share the same outcomes.

"Therefore, I believe that science sings with creation the majesty of God and His praises. Just look at the rain, the moon, and the rising sun. The flowers in the field that grow only by direction of their Creator." Christian concluded his argument and then turned to Willow. "I thank you for your time." He smiled and nodded in her direction.

"Good morning, class, Mrs. Wilson, and Christian. Although Christian brings some interesting points to the discussion, I would like to argue the following. In 1859 Charles Darwin presented the theory that each creature goes through a series of evolutionary changes based on the following four stages: difference, birthright, choice, and time. These four pillars . . . "

As she spoke the words she'd so carefully rehearsed, there was another shift inside of her. Willow's stomach clenched and her voice stuck in her throat. This wasn't right and she couldn't pretend that it was. Even as she glanced down at her notes, the obvious flaws in her argument stood out in sharp contrast to the truth she now knew. Taking a deep breath, she stopped. It would probably cost her grade, but she wouldn't hide anymore.

Pushing her shoulders back and standing up straight, she said, "My name is Willow Rysen." Those who knew the old Willow chuckled, waiting for whatever stunt she would pull next. But she focused on Christian. His face gave her courage. "I know that most of you think you know me. In fact, some have shared in the pranks I've pulled over the past few years." She inwardly cringed, the shame she felt pressing her to continue. "Some of you have been on the receiving end of those pranks, and I have probably spread untrue rumors about some of you." A single tear slid down her cheek.

Now for the hard part.

She braced herself against the podium. "I'm sorry." Audible gasps filled the class, but Willow pushed on. "I'm sorry if I teased you and made you feel like you didn't matter. I'm sorry if I hurt you with my words or if the pranks I pulled embarrassed you. I don't believe the Bible is a lie anymore. I don't believe science has the right to question the Bible either. I've learned how small I am when it comes to God. He is so much more than anyone here could've imagined, and He wants to come into each one of your lives and make you new." Her voice trailed off to little more than a whisper, and she stared at Christian, hoping he would recognize these next words were for him. "Most of all, I'm sorry that none of this in any way makes up for how I've treated you. I'll regret that mistake for the rest of my life." With that, Willow ran over to her desk, slipped her bag over her shoulder, and left the classroom.

She'd done it.

Her chest felt tight, and her heart beat heavily against her breastbone. The blue linoleum became a blur as she sought the direction of the office.

"Can I help you, honey?" Mrs. Fredrick, the office assistant, glanced up at Willow. Her eyes filled with compassion when she saw her weepy eyes.

"P—please will you p—phone my mom. I really need to go home," Willow murmured, fresh tears running down her face.

"Sure, honey, just a minute. Take a seat in the waiting room."

Willow walked out of the office and sank into a chair.

"Willow? Are you okay?"

Willow sniffed and looked up. Christian's best friend sat nearby. "Jack. What are you doing here?"

Jack rested a big hand on her shoulder. "I'm on my way to Phillips, but it can wait for a minute." He squeezed her shoulder. "He cares, you know."

Willow's heart stopped. She stared at Jack, not sure if she could believe what he'd said. But something like sunlight sparkled in her heart. "Are you sure?" she whispered. Could it be true?

"I've known Christian for years. He's head over heels for you."

Mrs. Frederick came into the waiting room. "Willow, I spoke to your mom. It's okay for you to go home."

Willow wiped her tears. "Thank you." She turned to Jack and offered him one last smile. "Thank you, too." She then hurried out to her car. She would have to explain herself to her mom, but right now, she didn't want to think at all.

SEVENTEEN

A stunned silence overtook the room. Everyone glanced around then as if by collective agreement erupted in a cacophony of voices.

"Now, settle down," Mrs. Wilson called. "Paulette and Taylor, you're up next." Mrs. Wilson walked over to the large white intercom stuck on the far wall of the classroom. She pressed the speak button. "Mrs. Frederick, do you perhaps know where Willow Rysen went?"

"She's here at the office."

"Thank you. Right. Paulette and Taylor, you have the floor."

Christian returned to his seat and closed his eyes. *Thank You, God,* he whispered. Willow had found her way after all. His mind wandered back to the looks he and Willow had shared, the relief on her face when he'd walked up to her this morning. The new Willow had come out of the old one and decided to make a stand. What did that mean for them? Was there hope for his foolish heart after all?

When the bell rang, Christian grabbed his books and dove for the door. He needed to find Willow. There was so much he needed to tell her.

A large hand clamped on his shoulder and stopped him in his tracks. "She went home. But I think you need to call her after school." Jack steered Christian in the direction of their math class.

"Why?"

"Just do it. I'm sure it'll work out." Jack smiled mysteriously and sat at his desk. Christian walked over to his. What was Jack going on about? Was this the sign he'd been waiting for?

The day passed as a blur. Rumors buzzed around the school, and he hoped that she was prepared for what was to come.

When the last bell finally rang, Christian rushed out to his car and drove home.

His mom stood in the kitchen as the front door clattered closed behind him.

"Christian, is that you?"

Christian threw his bag on the nearby couch. "You'll never believe what happened today at school. Willow stood up in our debate, told the whole class that her side of the disagreement was rubbish, then apologized to everyone for hurting them."

His mother chuckled quietly. "And?"

Christian's face heated. "And she said she was sorry for the way she treated me in the past. At least I think that's what she meant to say. Jack told me to call her. What do you think?"

His mother rested the knife on the counter next to the carrots she'd been chopping. "Well, Christian, I think the real question is what do you think?"

"I honestly don't know, Mom. You should have seen her today, all scared and unsure. It was like she was different person. And there's this peace in her eyes I've never seen. It makes her so beautiful." His mother raised a knowing eyebrow, and his face flushed. "Mom, I—"

"Christian, I know. If this is the girl for you, pray about it and then trust that God will work it out. But don't be scared of your own doubt."

Taking his mom's advice with him, Christian went up to his room and sat on the edge of his bed, his phone between his open hands. Nerves chewed his stomach, and he felt slightly nauseous. What if Jack misunderstood? Or what if he was joking?

Jack would never joke about something as serious as this. His hands shook so badly that he could barely hold his phone in his hands. Was he ready for what this might mean? Stilling his hands with his resolve, he opened his texting app.

Thatboy: Hi, Willow, it's Christian.

He waited. Would she answer this time? After that first day, he'd sent numerous messages, but all of them had come back unread.

Populargirl: Hi. You spoke to Jack?

Christian smiled, relief releasing the tension in his shoulders, and he flopped back onto his bed.

Thatboy: Yeah. Are you okay?

Populargirl: Awful.

Thatboy: You want to get together and talk about it?

Christian held his breath. Would Willow want to talk to him? She seemed to have been doing her best to avoid him all this time. The three blue dots came onto the messenger screen.

Populargirl: Don't know . . .

Thatboy: Please talk to me.

There was a long pause before another message came through.

Populargirl: Why would you want anything to do with a girl like me? I'm so messed up.

Christian took a deep breath. Well, it was now or never.

Thatboy: Willow, I like you.

Christian's heart thrashed wildly in his chest as he hit the send button. Maybe it was too soon or maybe he was just crazy enough about Willow to put himself out there. Needing something to do with his hands, he went downstairs to the kitchen. His mom was in the study working on her latest sewing project. Grabbing a few sandwich ingredients from the fridge, his phone buzzed in his pocket again. He set the ingredients on the counter and looked at the message.

Populargirl: I like you, too. Can I meet you later?

Christian read the words a few times before their meaning sunk in. Willow felt the same. A slow smile spread across his face, and something warm beat in his chest. Leaning against the counter, he scrubbed his face with his hands.

Thatboy: Sure. Do you want to come over? My mom won't mind. Or should I come to you?

Carefully preparing his sandwich, he waited for Willow's answer knowing that if he sat still the anxiety might give him a heart attack. Was this really happening?

Populargirl: I think it's better if I come to you. Are you sure your mom won't mind?

Thatboy: I'm sure.

Populargirl: I'll be over soon.

Christian's smile grew then his nerves kicked in. After pushing all the mess from his sandwich into their places, he hurried to the study.

He gently knocked on the door frame. "Mom, are you busy?"

The whir of the sewing machine came to a halt, and his mom turned around to face him. "Do you need something?"

"Is it okay if Willow comes over?"

His mom's eyes went wide. "The girl you like?"

"Yeah."

"Okay, I have to say I've been looking forward to seeing this girl who has you all tangled in knots again."

Christian felt his neck heat. After planting a quick kiss on her soft cheek, he rushed upstairs to take a shower and change his clothes. He'd just sat down to tie his shoes when the doorbell pealed through the stillness of the house. Christian wiped his hands on his jeans and took a deep breath, silently lamenting the fact that there wasn't something that could slow down his heart rate. Hurrying down the stairs, he paused for a moment. The front door clicked faintly.

"Willow, it's so lovely to see you again," his mother said.

Christian hurried down the rest of the stairs, his breath catching. The soft pink of Willow's sweater against her dark hair made her look fragile and delicate.

"Susan, I would really like to apologize for what happened the last time I was in your house."

His mom shook her head and smiled. "It's in the past." His mom stepped forward and engulfed Willow in a tight hug. "Welcome to the family of God."

Willow stiffened in surprise and then her wet eyes caught his over his mom's shoulder. "Thank you," she whispered.

His mom stepped back. "I hope we will be seeing more of you from now on."

Willow's blue eyes met his in question. Willow laughed. "I hope so, too."

"Come on, we can talk in the den." Unable to be so far from her anymore Christian took her hand into his, a shiver racing up his spine.

His mom smiled and raised her eyebrows knowingly then stepped back into the study.

Christian led Willow down the stairs into the den, the dim light becoming brighter as he flicked on the lamp.

"Have a seat." He gestured to the couch.

Willow shifted in the doorway, her expression unsure and her eyes troubled.

"What's the matter?"

A sob spurred Christian into action. In an instant, he was at the door and Willow was in his arms. "What's going on?" he whispered.

Willow sniffed gently, pressing away from him. "I'm sorry. I'm so sorry for the way I treated you." Christian pulled her close again, settling his chin on top of her soft head. Willow continued, "There is so much to say, to explain."

Pulling her with him, Christian settled them on a nearby sofa. He handed Willow a fresh batch of tissues and dabbed the flow on her cheeks. "Hey, it's okay." He drew her close again.

After a few deep breaths, Willow composed herself enough to speak. "That day in the library made me feel things I'd never felt before. Things that scared me. What scared me more was that if I chose to be with you, I would have to give up everything I was." She leaned her head on his shoulder and stared down at her hands. "This weekend, I decided to give God my all, no matter the cost. Felicia reacted like I thought she would when I told her. I doubt we will be friends ever again, but you know, it was worth it. For the first time in my life I feel at peace with myself. I feel free." The peace that he'd seen in Willow's eyes earlier filled them again. Her tentative smile slowly spread until it grew wide.

"Willow, when you gave your life to Jesus, He forgave you," Christian said. "All that stuff you did has been forgiven. And I forgive you, too. I meant what I said earlier. I like you. I didn't understand how I could be drawn to you, but the more time we spent together, the more I wanted to be with you."

For a moment he just stared at her, his heart beating hard with anticipation. Willow's eyes fluttered closed and that was all the invitation he needed. When his lips met hers, he knew that he was falling in love with Willow Rysen.

Willow melted into the kiss, her legs going weak at the knees. It was unlike any kiss she'd ever experienced. It was pure, fresh, and gentle like the man giving it.

After a long moment, Christian ended the kiss. Both breathed hard as he laid his forehead against hers.

"My reputation at school is greatly overexaggerated," she said. She felt a need for him to know the truth. To know everything. "I mean, the alcohol and stupidity is pretty accurate, but most of what you've heard is made up. You say you forgive me, but what happens when you're reminded of those things that I have done? What then?"

"I'll admit, I haven't really thought about it."

"There's no competition," she said. "I mean between you and the other guys."

"It doesn't change how I feel about you, you know."

Willow shivered. "You're sure?"

Christian nodded. "Not a bit."

EIGHTEEN

Christian took a deep breath and stared out his car door at Willow's house. Was this really happening? Had last night been real?

Steadying his breathing, he climbed out of the car and swiftly moved to the door. His hands shook with anxiety against the doorbell, making it sound a little sick. He waited. Then the most beautiful face stared shyly out from the open door and his anxiety disappeared.

"Hey, Christian, come in and meet my mom." Willow smiled, giving him a quick kiss before turning back into the house.

The dream continued and Christian followed her in.

"I need to get my bag then we can go," Willow said over her shoulder before hurrying up a flight of stairs.

Christian settled against the wall sliding his hands into his pockets.

"Well, hello there, you must be Christian?" an older woman walked down the stairs toward him.

Christian straightened and pulled his hands out of his pockets. "Yes, and you must be Willow's mom?"

The older lady smiled. She was Willow's beauty matured. "Willow has told me a lot about you."

"I hope all good?"

Mrs. Rysen chuckled. "Yes, more than you could know. I wanted to thank you for forcing my Willow to go that meeting. Her transformation has made me take a good look at our family again, and I want to thank you for that."

Amazement lanced through him. "I didn't do anything. God just used me as a messenger, and I am very grateful for that."

"You ready?" Willow called from upstairs.

"Whatever you did and didn't do, I am still grateful to have my little girl back," Mrs. Rysen said. "It was nice to meet you, Christian, don't be a stranger."

Willow hopped down the last stair, and Christian led her out to his car. "Is your mom a Christian?" he asked.

"You know what, she is. I found out only yesterday when I came home from school. We had a long discussion about it after I told her what happened at school. She hid it all these years because of my dad. Apparently, it used to cause huge arguments between them, so her faith became private. She even goes to Bible study with your mom."

"Wow."

The radio played softly in the background as they drove, and Willow sat oddly silent beside him.

"You okay?" he asked.

Willow smiled, her eyes troubled.

"You worried about Felicia?"

"Yes, we've been friends forever. I guess I just hoped . . . maybe she'll come around."

"It'll be okay. Do you want to sit with me at lunch?" he asked.

Willow giggled, the sound a bit hollow. "Are you sure your friends won't mind? After all this is me."

"It'll take some getting used to. Maybe we should find our own table."

"Yeah." Willow shifted her fingers again.

Christian reached over and gently unfolded her white-knuckled grip. "It'll be okay. I know Jack is okay with us at least."

Willow's smile was more relaxed now.

"There's a Bible study for new believers tonight at the church. Do you want to come?"

"Sure, that sounds great. What time?"

"It's at seven. Do you want me to come get you?"

"No, thanks. Mom and I are going out for dinner. I'm not sure what time we'll finish. Can I meet you there?"

"Sure, it's in the youth hall around the left side of the church."

He eased the car into his usual parking space and cut the engine. Willow's hand tensed in his, but a brave smile lingered on her mouth.

"You ready for this?" he said and pulled her closer, maybe a kiss would make her feel better? He pressed his lips against hers.

A slight giggle erupted against his mouth as someone thumped on the window. Christian pulled back to see Willow looking behind him.

"Hey, you two, get a room." Jack laughed. He yanked the door open and hauled Christian out of the car.

Ignoring Jack's curious eyes, Christian walked to the other side of the car and opened Willow's door. Her cheeks were still flushed with color, an easy smile on her face. He helped her out of the car, kissing her forehead as her body met his. Sliding his arm around Willow's waist, Christian walked her toward the school, stifling a chuckle at Jack's sly smile.

"You . . ." Jack began.

Christian shook his head. Jack knew him well enough to know that now was not the time to joke. There would be plenty of time when Willow was in class.

Loud gasps echoed in the hallway as Christian, Willow, and Jack entered the school building. Beside him, Willow blew out an irritated breath.

"I guess I should have expected this," she muttered and pressed closer into his side.

"Hey, just look at me and all will be well. I mean who wouldn't want to look at this face." He gestured modestly to himself.

Willow giggled, her irritated expression relaxing. She rose on her toes, grabbed his face, and gave him a quick kiss. There. Right before Jack and every other student in their school. The whispers reached fever pitch.

"I'll see you at lunch," Christian murmured.

Willow nodded. She nervously glanced inside the class.

Christian rubbed a hand down her arm. "It'll be okay. I'm praying for you." With one last kiss, he gently pushed her into the class then followed Jack to their own class.

"So, I gather everything worked out?" Jack pointed over his shoulder in the direction of Willow's class.

Christian nodded. "Yesterday, we talked, and she stayed for dinner. Met mom and dad. I met her mom this morning. Man, I still think I'm in a dream."

"I'm happy for you man. Even if it has to be Willow Rysen," he teased.

When at last the lunch bell rang, Christian was more than ready to see Willow. His footsteps came to sudden halt as he rounded the corner, raised voices meeting him.

"Willow, what's happened to you? Is this some kind of joke?"

"Felicia, you know me better than anyone. Would I really make up something like this?"

"Yeah, you would. You've always done what you've wanted no matter who it hurt."

Willow sighed. "Yes, you're right. I'm sorry."

"I don't want your apology. Perhaps you've fooled that guy you're so fascinated with, but you can't fool me."

"This is for real. I've changed."

"Spell me another one, Willow. For as long as I've known you, it's always been about what makes you happy, how can you one up the next guy, who you have to step over to get what you want. I don't believe this God thing for a second."

Willow's face flushed, and she hung her head. Christian crossed over to them and gently touched the small of Willow's back. She sagged against his hand.

"Everything okay here?" He looked down at Willow's troubled face.

Felicia's expression hardened. "What do you want, Nerd Boy?"

"That's enough, Felicia," Willow said.

Contempt filled Felicia's hard expression. "If this is what you want, Will, I don't see anything else to discuss." She then spun on her heel in the direction of the lunchroom.

"Oh, Willow, I'm sorry." Christian wrapped his arms around Willow's shaking form. Tears soaked the front of his t-shirt. "It'll be all right. Somehow."

Willow wiped her eyes and nodded.

"Outside?" Christian asked. It was still cold, the spring having not fully shed its winter wings, but right now, anything would be better for Willow than sitting in the same room as Felicia Wren and her group of friends.

"I'm not really hungry anyway."

Together, they walked down the lunch line and out the door into the sunny afternoon. They sat down on a bench.

"Thank you for standing up for me." Willow shifted closer to him and rested her head on his shoulder.

"Anytime." And he placed another sweet kiss on her cheek.

The bed sagged under her weight as she fell into it. If she was totally honest with herself, what had she really expected from Felicia? Felicia wouldn't see anything different from her behavior until she proved it to her. Willow sighed. Even another apology wouldn't help, not that she wouldn't try. She would. Rolling onto her stomach, she reached for the leather Bible beside her bed. Tenderly lifting the pages, she read one of her mom's favorite verses:

> *Psalm 23:4. Even though I walk through the darkest valley, I will fear no evil, for you are with me; your rod and your staff, they comfort me.*

Today had felt like a dark valley. Although even when she was alone, she'd felt a strength and determination that she was sure hadn't come from her.

Bowing her head, she thanked God for keeping her and being with her during the day.

"Willow," her mom called.

"Coming." Willow jumped off her bed and hurried down the stairs into the living room.

"I'm on my way," Mom said, meeting Willow at the bottom of the stairs. She stopped. "Are you okay?"

Willow walked into her mother's hug. "It's been a rough day."

"Just remember, God is with you always, even when it feels like you are alone."

Willow smiled. She was sure her mom knew from experience. "Thanks, Mom."

"The errand shouldn't take long. I'll be there as soon as I can. I love you." Her mom hurried out of the house.

"I love you, too, Mom." Willow took a deep breath then finished readying for her night. Thirty minutes later, she was on her way to the restaurant. Bringing the car to a gentle stop at the red light, Willow studied the busy road. The afternoon traffic was slowly finding its way home, and the roads were beginning to clear.

The light turned green, and she pushed the accelerator. The car slid forward. Tires screeched to her left. A large truck skipped through the red traffic light and sped toward her. Willow's heart lurched in her chest. Something hard struck her car. The light faded then everything went black.

NINETEEN

"Did you invite Willow?" His mom packed a plate of brownie squares into the cooler.

"Yeah, she said she'll meet me there. Her and her mom had a dinner date."

His mom smiled. "That sounds lovely. Gloria has spoken often of Willow. I didn't realize that her Willow and your Willow were the same girl. I should have. I mean how many Willows could there be in Bethel?"

The lilting melody of "Blue Danube" rang from his mom's phone. She glanced down at it, a frown crossing her brow. "Hi, Gloria, how are you?" Her friendly smile fell into a deep frown. Slowly, her pink cheeks turned white. "We will be there soon." She ended the call, licked her lips, and turned her gaze on Christian. "Willow has been in an accident."

Shock skittered through Christian's body.

"Christian," his mom called. Her voice sounded far away.

"Christian."

His brain shouted instructions, but his mouth refused to open and respond.

"Christian, we need to get to the hospital."

Finally, he nodded. Somehow, he ended up in the car, his heart rioting in his chest, his brain numb.

The drive to hospital was short. Once they arrived, he climbed out of the car. The harsh lights flashing around the hospital parking lot snapped reality back in his face. Christian gasped. *God help me,* he cried inside, trying to push past the numbness. With unsteady legs, Christian followed his parents into the emergency waiting area. Doctors and nurses ran here and there through the emergency area, voices buzzing, some loud, some soft. A woman stood by the reception desk, her expression haggard. Her gaze turned to Christian and his parents.

"Susan." Willow's mom ran toward them. The two women embraced, tears leaking down their cheeks. Mrs. Rysen pulled back from his mom, her expression strained. "We don't know anything yet. The nurse says she in surgery."

"Does anyone know what happened?" his mom asked.

"Why don't we go to the waiting room, and I'll tell you what I know." Mrs. Rysen led the way out of the reception area to a small waiting room down the hall.

A man sat with his head in his hands and his shoulders hunched on a light-colored sofa in the corner. He raised his head as they walked in.

"Dan, this is Susan, she's a friend of mine and this is her family," Mrs. Rysen said. "Her son Christian is friends with Willow from school." Mrs. Rysen's eyes begged him not to refute her story. He glanced at his mom and acknowledged her small nod. Mrs. Rysen smiled, gratefully twisting her hands together. Then she said, "When I arrived at the restaurant for my dinner date with Willow, she hadn't arrived. I tried to call her phone a few times, and eventually, someone picked it up. It was one of the deputies from the county sheriff department. He was at the scene of a horrific car accident. He asked me for a description of Willow then said that it matched the description of the person who had been taken away by ambulance." Heavy tears splashed onto Mrs. Rysen's tight fingers. "A drunk driver hit Willow's car, pushing it into a nearby field. The car rolled twice before striking a tree at the edge of the field." Sobs broke off Mrs. Rysen's words.

Hot, wetness slid down Christian's cheeks, something cracking inside him. He pressed his palms against his eyes and lowered himself into a chair. *Father, help her please*, he prayed again and again.

After what seemed like hours, a tired looking lady wearing blue scrubs entered the room. "Mr. and Mrs. Rysen?"

"Yes." Mrs. Rysen jumped to her feet.

"Willow has taken a severe blow to the head. There are two fractures to her spine, and there is a good possibility that her spleen has been ruptured."

The nurse's words faded into blackness. Christian blinked hard a few times to concentrate on what she was saying, but all he could think was, *why, Lord?* He and Willow had just found each other. Why now?

"Christian, it's okay. Willow is going to make it." His mother's calm voice penetrated his fuzzy thoughts.

Relief pierced the darkness, and hope took flight. *Please help her.* Hands rested on his shoulders again, and his father's low voice pled for Willow's life and healing, his words softly echoed by his mom.

Another hour went by.

Then another. Doctors were working on Willow's spine.

And another. His mom continued praying softly.

Five hours later, the nurse came back into the room. "Willow made it through the surgery, but she's in a coma."

Relief mingled with concern was written on each person's face. Mrs. Rysen softly wept in Mr. Rysen's arms. Christian felt like weeping himself, but he had to hold it together for Willow. He swallowed and harshly shut the flood gates. God was a God of miracles. Willow had to make it out.

A silent hour later, a tall man in green scrubs and smelling of antiseptic walked into the room. "Mr. and Mrs. Rysen?" he asked.

At Mrs. Rysen's nod, the man sat in a chair across from them. "I'm Dr. Thomas, Willow's surgeon. Willow is responding well to treatment, and her condition is stable. We've managed to sew up her cuts, and we've done what we can for the injuries to her back. Only time will tell how severe those injuries were and the long-term ramifications. Right now, all she needs is rest, and if you are praying people, a lot of prayer."

"Will she walk again?" Mr. Rysen asked.

The doctor shook his head. "At this stage, nothing is certain. We can only wait and see."

"Thank you, Doctor." Mrs. Rysen stood to shake the doctor's hand.

"One more thing. A head trauma of this nature often causes amnesia. The amnesia could be slight or nonexistent. But again, as I said, nothing is certain right now."

"Can I see her?" Christian blurted out.

Mr. Rysen threw him an angry look. "Now, Christian, I don't think—"

"It's okay, Dan. She means a great deal to him," Mrs. Rysen said. "We'll see her first."

"Only for a few minutes." The doctor escorted Mr. and Mrs. Rysen to Willow's room.

Christian followed closely behind, his heart heavy, his hands and jaw aching from clenching them. His high emotions teetered on the edge of a precipice, and he swallowed hard against their onslaught. Impatiently, he leaned against the wall waiting for Mr. and Mrs. Rysen to come out. *God, please let her be all right.*

TWENTY

The hallway had the starkness that one would expect from a hospital—white walls, white floors, and florescent lights that hung from the roof. Dread whistled through Christian like a tornado on its path of destruction.

At last, the door opened.

Pale light emitted into the bleak corridor, and Mr. and Mrs. Rysen shuffled out. A gentle hand touched his, and he glanced up to Mrs. Rysen's face. The pain he saw there hit in the stomach. Whatever Willow's parents had seen was a lot worse than they'd expected.

Saying one more silent prayer, Christian braced himself and walked into the room. Willow's room was white, sterile, and smelled like Dr. Thomas. A low light glowed in the dim interior, and the lone sound of a faint beep broke the deadly silence. In the middle of the room, Willow lay in bed, the paleness in her cheeks illuminated by the rich, darkness of her hair.

His knees folded beneath him, and he stumbled his way to her bedside. Tears blurred the tubes that ran out of her body and the huge white bandage that covered half her head. She lay so still that if not for the moving of her chest, he would've thought he'd lost her. Christian took her hand into his. It felt cold compared to the warm vibrant hands he'd remembered holding at school that day. Tears cascaded down his face, the last of his control gone. *Oh, God, please, help her.*

"Please come back to me," he whispered. Christian laid his head beside hers and wept.

The days passed slowly. For the first few days after the accident, Christian stayed home from school, the pain and devastation leaving him in a semi-catatonic state. All he could think about, focus on, and dream about was Willow. Each day he would go to the hospital and sit by her bedside, whispering to her how much he loved and missed her, how glad he was that she'd found God, and how much he wanted her to come back to him.

The days turned to weeks and the time came for Christian to return to school.

"Mr. Blythe, where is yesterday's homework?" Mrs. Suarez asked for the fourth time that day.

Christian stared at her. He was sure he'd done the homework.

For the first time in his life, Christian made his way down the hallway to Principal Rory's office, and this time it wasn't to receive an accolade.

Scrubbing his hand through his hair, Christian cleared his throat then knocked on the door of the Principal's office.

"Enter."

Christian pushed the door open, his heart galloping in his chest.

"Ah, Christian." Principal Rory clasped his hands on his desk. His deep brown eyes spoke of years of intelligence and a habit of not taking nonsense. The streaks of gray in his black hair usually gave him a distinguished air, but today, it made him look intimidating.

"Come in. Sit down."

"Yes, sir." Christian quietly closed the door behind him and sat on the black chair beside a large smooth table.

"Christian, do you want to tell me what's going on with you?" he asked.

Christian took a deep breath and quickly explained the accident and Willow and how he felt about it all.

Principal Rory slowly nodded, his expression filled with understanding. "Well, Christian, it sounds to me like you are struggling to deal with this particular situation."

"Sir, one thing I'm struggling to understand is why? Why now? I mean Willow just got right with God and things started going well between us. Why did she have to be in the accident?" He stared at the man across the table.

"Are you a believer?"

"Yes, a recent one."

A small sympathetic smile broke out on Principal Rory's face. "God's ways are not always our ways. Sometimes it's hard to understand why He allows things to happen but know that God always has some good planned from it. There is a verse in Romans 8:28 that says, 'And we know that in all things God works for the good of those who love him, who have been called according to his purpose.' Hold onto faith, Christian. Following God doesn't mean that life will be easy, but it does mean that no matter what happens, God is with us."

"Thank you, sir," Christian whispered.

"Now, let's try get those assignments in on time. Okay?" Principal Rory smiled.

Taking his bag, Christian nodded and stood. "Yes, sir."

Christian hurried out of the room and crashed into someone.

"Hey, watch it!" a girl shrieked.

"Felicia, man, I'm sorry. I didn't see you there," Christian said, taking a step back.

Felicia crossed her arms over her chest, the sneer in her face falling into a different expression.

Christian raised an eyebrow then shook his head and tightened his hold on his bag. "I'll see you around."

"Wait a minute," Felicia said. "How is Willow?"

"She's okay. Still in a coma. Did you speak to Mrs. Rysen?"

"Yeah, she said about the same. I was hoping . . . I don't know . . . that you would say something different."

Christian shook his head. "I wish I had better news. I know Willow would love to see you, you know."

"Yeah, maybe. Anyway, I'll see you around."

"See you."

Felicia walked away, her shoulders hunched.

The weeks turned to months, and Willow still slept on.

Christian visited each day, convinced that one day Willow would open her eyes while he was there. The last weeks of school flew by, and before he knew it, he was graduating high school without Willow.

"Christian Blythe," Principal Rory announced.

Christian stood from his chair and walked to the stage, taking his diploma. He pasted a brave smile on his face. Instead of feeling a sense of finality, he only felt hollow. He followed his feet down the stairs of the stage and out of Bethel Private School. That chapter of his life was over, yet strings held him fast to it all because of Willow.

TWENTY-ONE

The next morning, his phone rang early.

"Jack, do you have any idea what time it is?" he growled into the phone, rubbing the sleep from his eyes.

"Come on, you and I both know you weren't sleeping."

"Is there a reason you're bothering my non-sleep?"

Jack laughed. "Actually, yes, I have an idea."

"I'm listening. Against my will, but I'm listening."

"Come with me to Westwood. I spoke to Mom, and she organized everything. I leave tomorrow morning. We'll have some fun in the sun."

"Jack, I need to stay here with Willow."

"Dude, Westwood is only a couple of hours drive and less than that by plane. If she wakes up, you can be back before you know it. Come on, man, you and I both need a break."

Jack's words made sense. Maybe going somewhere was better than just sitting around waiting. He'd lost count of the number of times his mom had encouraged him to go out, do something, see people.

"Okay, I'll talk to my folks."

"Excellent. Let me know."

Christian threw the phone onto his bed and sagged back against his pillows. Did he sit here and wait for Willow, hoping against hope that she would wake up? Or did he go with Jack and enjoy the summer? Indecision swirled in his mind. *What do You think, God?*

"Christian, are you up?" his mom called.

"I am now, thanks to Jack."

Noting his acerbic tone, his mom came into his room. "Something wrong?"

"Other than the obvious?" Maybe he did need some time away. "Sorry, Mom, I didn't mean that. Jack called and asked if I wanted to go with him to Westwood."

"Yes, Lily and I spoke about it. He needs to go find himself or some such nonsense."

"He didn't say that, but do you think I should go?"

"Christian, you're past the age where I should be making the decision for you. As your mother, I think that maybe some time away would put things into perspective for you. And it might give the distance you need to consider your future and how Willow will fit into it. I know you want to be here when she wakes up, but life doesn't stand still even if someone we love is in a coma." His mom gathered up the laundry and walked out of the room, leaving him to his thoughts.

For a long while, he stared blankly at the ceiling, a battle inside him. One side told him to go and get away. The other shouted the what ifs. What if something happened to Willow and he was unable to get back? What if she woke up and he wasn't there?

What if you just trusted Me? A voice spoke into his heart loud and clear. Shooting up into a sitting position, he looked around the room, sure that the voice had come from somewhere else. There was no one else in the room with him. Christian closed his eyes. *God is that You?*

Trust Me. The words came again.

Willow was in God's hands, and whether he was in Westwood or Bethel, God would be with her.

Swiping open his phone, he opened his messenger app and sent Jack a quick text. Tomorrow, he would be going to Westwood.

An hour later, he walked into Willow's room. The resolve he'd held for the past few hours almost crumbled at the sight of her beautiful form. Her cheeks that had been stark white were now filled with a bit more color. The gray tone of her skin more normal, her chest moving in the same rhythm as the machines.

"Hi, Willow," he said, pulling the familiar blue chair closer to the side of her bed. He lifted her hand and ran his fingers over the rise of her knuckles, the blue lines of her veins. His heart clenched painfully. "Please come back to me."

The idea of leaving her ripped through him. Maybe going with Jack wasn't such a good idea. *Trust Me,* the voice whispered softly inside him. Sighing, he kissed Willow's hand, then he stood up and kissed her forehead. "Goodbye, my love." He closed the door gently behind him. *God please make her well.*

TWENTY-TWO

It's strange how clear the sky is here, Christian thought, staring over the bustling waves. The sound of voices and music came from somewhere in the distance. They'd been in Westwood for almost a week, and Christian was slowly relaxing from the stress of the past few weeks. Some days he felt guilty about being there and other days he felt like he could breath again. He missed Willow fiercely, but the time away with Jack had taught him patience and perseverance every day. Breathing in the salty air, he let his mind wander through his memories.

"Dude, we're leaving." Jack stormed over to Christian, his face a dark mask of anger. His body vibrated with some kind of urgency and a deep pain bled from his gaze.

"You okay, man?" he asked.

Jack's shoulders stiffened further. "Fine." Although his tone said he was anything but. "You ready to go?"

Christian took one more look at the cresting waves, the blue waters reminding him of Willow's eyes. "Yeah, all good."

Jack just turned and walked into the covering darkness. As if by silent agreement, they walked back to the place they were staying. Judging by the range of emotions displayed in his expression, Jack seemed to be arguing with some voice in his head.

"Jack, are you okay?" Christian pushed the unlocked door open.

"What? Yeah. Fine." Jack's eyes unfocused again like he was lost in some unpleasant memory or moment.

"You want to talk about it?"

Jack ran a hand through his hair. "No, no. How could she? It wouldn't do . . ." He disappeared down the hallway to his room, the door clicking closed.

Christian stared after him. What on earth had happened at the beach?

Christian shook his head and went to bed, hoping that tonight at least his dreams would be pleasant. Tomorrow, he'd try to figure out what had happened to Jack.

He stood at the bottom of a large, grass covered hill, the smell of honeysuckle thick in the air. Christian closed his eyes and opened his arms, enjoying the cool breeze that blew into him. When he opened his eyes, there was someone at the top of the hill. Her chestnut hair fluttered in the breeze and her white dress swirled around her knees. Her blue eyes were alive and warm with happiness.

"Christian," she called out to him, beckoning him closer.

Almost overcome with emotion, Christian ran up the hill; however, with each step he took, Willow seemed to be further away.

"Christian," she called again, her voice becoming urgent.

He ran harder and harder, his breath panting out in deep gasps by the time he reached her.

"Willow," he whispered. Burying his face into her hair, the sweet smell of Willow surrounded him. He tightened his embrace. How he'd missed her.

"Come home," she said.

Christian jolted awake. It had been so real. He was sure Willow had been there right beside him. He could feel her sweet breath blowing on his shoulder. Reality crashed down on him, and a tear trickled down his face. It was the first time that he'd had this dream about Willow since leaving Bethel. The pain he'd felt at leaving intensified. He didn't know how much longer he could hold on until his heart finally broke. Was Willow ever going to come back to him?

The thought stayed with him as the darkness of sleep slipped back over him. His mind alert as the dream pulled him in again. Again and again the dream repeated until finally the sound of a calypso beat ripped him sweating and gasping into reality. Stunned by the sudden intrusion, Christian looked around the room. The walls and decor looked the same, the blue and white comforter that was his looked normal, although somewhat rumpled, but he couldn't shake the feeling that something had changed. Something major.

TWENTY-THREE

Something warm burned her face. Willow tried to lift her hand to touch her cheek. Did she leave the curtains open again when she'd gone to bed last night? Blinking hard, she pushed apart her sticky eyelids only to close them again against the bright light. She really needed to close that curtain. Slowly opening her eyes again, she looked around the room.

The comforter on her bed was the wrong color, and she was sure if she moved a little to the left, she would fall off her bed. A large bouquet of yellow roses stood on the table beside her head, their color bright against the white walls and ceiling. And the blue chair. She would never have that in her room. Where was she?

The faint sound of beeping turned her head again, the lines on the monitor next to her jumping in time with her racing heart. Placing her hands beside her, she tried to push herself into a seated position only to flop back down on the bed, her elbow landing hard on something solid. A small flick of pain wormed up her arm. What was wrong with her arms? Gasping from the effort it took to lift them, she studied their emaciated appearance. What had happened to her?

The door flew open, and a surprised lady with deep brown eyes stared back at her. "Hello, Willow." The friendly smile instantly put

Willow's frantic heart rate at ease. "My name is Mattie. I'm your nurse. Welcome back."

Willow licked her lips, but she couldn't seem to get her mouth to form the words she wanted to say.

Mattie's smile didn't waver. "Why don't you just lie back down, and I'll call your ma and pa."

Willow nodded, well, at least she tried to. There seemed to be something wrong with her neck, too. Mattie pressed a button on the side of the bed and lifted Willow's body up. "That should help ya get comfortable. Now ya just hold on, and I'll be right back."

Willow's gaze rested on a large book that looked out of place on the bedside table. Willow pulled it on her lap, feeling the soft pages rustle against her fingertips. There was a long list of names on the first few pages. Something about the word Genesis struck a chord in her, hinting on a memory, but as fleetingly as it came, it disappeared again. Tiredness weighed down her eyes and limbs, and she let herself pass into darkness again.

The sun was in a different place when she opened her eyes.

"Willow." She knew that voice. It was her mother's voice.

"M—mom?" She forced open her eyes. This time, they adjusted easily to the sunshine bursting through the window.

"Oh, my girl," her mother said. For some reason, it sounded like she'd been crying.

Willow's hand was engulfed in a warm one. She blinked a few times, her eyes finally focusing on the faces of her mom and dad. They both looked happy, so why were they crying?

The confusing moment was interrupted by the arrival of man dressed like a doctor.

"It looks like our patient is finally awake. Hi, Willow. I'm Dr. Thompson." The man smiled down at her.

"H—hi."

Dr. Thompson took a small penlight out of his pocket and shone it in her eyes. "Willow, what day is it today?" He flicked the light between her eyes.

Willow unwillingly followed the light. "Saturday, I think," she said.

Mattie slapped a blood pressure cuff onto her arm as Dr. Thompson took her wrist.

"What did you do today?" he asked.

The memories were a bit fuzzy and she struggled to line them up. "I went to ch—church with Christian for s—science."

"Do you remember anything about what happened there?"

Willow remembered the service but couldn't quite put her finger on what had gone on there. Then there was this fuzzy image of Felicia and a party. She closed her eyes, carefully focusing on the images flitting through her memory. There was a car, and a cliff, and somehow Christian was in there. What had she been doing with him?

"Not much," she said slowly.

Her mom and dad glanced at each other again.

Dr. Thompson finished up the exam. "Mr. and Mrs. Rysen, could I speak to you outside for a moment?"

"Now don't you worry, honey." Mattie drew back the rest of the curtains to let in the sunlight. "It'll all be okay."

Willow wasn't sure. There was something she was missing, something important. It beat in her very heart, but for the life of her, she couldn't remember what it was.

Mattie resettled her comforter around her, humming a happy tune as she tidied the room.

"Is that yours?" She pointed to the book resting on Willow's lap.

"I d—don't know," Willow said, opening the book.

Her hand landed on the dedication page.

My dearest Willow,

The decision you have made today made me the proudest mother in the world. I know that we haven't always been on the best terms, but from now on, with God's help, I hope that we can have a deep and special relationship as mother and daughter. Read this book, take its words to heart, and always trust the Lord in all you do.

All my love,

Mom

The letter and dedication were dated May, but it was only April.

"What is the date today?"

"Why it's the twenty fifth of July. The fall will be here soon."

"W—what," she gasped. Her body threatened to pull her back into sleep, but she needed to stay awake until her parents returned. She needed answers. She lifted the book closer to her face. A Bible. Why would her mother have given her a Bible? Flipping the pages through her fingers, she landed on a page that had a verse underlined in bright pink marker:

For God so loved the world that he gave his one and only Son, that whoever believes in him shall not perish but have eternal life. John 3:16

The words *For me* were written next to the verse in her distinctive scrawl.

Written underneath the verse was another: Ephesians 2:8. Willow quickly turned to the reference. Her fingers ran over the books like they knew where they were going. She found the reference and read:

For it is by grace you have been saved, through faith—and this is not from yourselves, it is the gift of God.

Snippets of a man ran through her memory. Pastor George she thought his name was. Yes, he'd been speaking that night. She remembered a prayer he'd spoken. Quieting her anxious spirit, Willow closed her eyes and bowed her head, praying the words that felt both foreign and familiar coming from her heart. "Dear Lord Jesus, please forgive my sins and come into my life. I'm sorry for the bad stuff I've done. I want to live for You, please come and be ruler of my heart. Amen."

A deep peace took up residence inside her. It felt like coming home into the deep embrace of Someone Who loved unconditionally. This time, Willow was grateful when sleep took her because she knew it would all work out for good.

TWENTY-FOUR

H is phone rang again as Christian stepped out of the shower.

"All right, all right, keep your shirt on. I'm coming," he muttered.

Five missed calls from his mother all within the last ten minutes. Anxiety seized his heart. Something was wrong. Willow. Drying off quickly, he slipped on a pair of pants and hit the redial button.

"Christian, where have you been?" his mother asked. There was something strange in her voice.

"I was in the shower. Is everything all right? Willow?"

He heard a sob catch in the background and then a shuffle.

"Christian, Willow's awake," his dad said.

If Bigfoot had chosen that moment to step out of hiding in front of him, Christian would have just stared with his mouth open. He stumbled back, the edge of the bed hitting his knees before he toppled down onto it. A flash of sunlight and happiness crashed into the darkness that had held him since the day of Willow's accident. It was the feeling of spring, the feeling of hope.

"Christian, did you hear what I said? Willow is awake," his father said with obvious elation.

"Th—that's great news," Christian responded, his mind whirring.

"How soon can you get home?" his dad asked.

"I'll need to catch a flight. Give me thirty minutes to make plans then I'll get back to you."

He needed to get home fast. Jumping up from his bed, he pulled out his laptop.

"Where's the fire, man?" Jack strolled into his room, eating a banana.

"Willow's awake." Christian lifted the laptop lid and quickly booted the machine, praying that the connection would be quick today.

"Wait, Willow's awake?" Jack lowered the banana from his mouth.

Christian gave a distracted nod and quickly scanned the airline's web page. There were no flights over the next few days. Christian's heart sank. He should've known something like this would happen. He should've stayed in Bethel.

"What's wrong?" Jack sat at the end of Christian's bed.

"There aren't any flights out in the next few days."

"So, take the car." Jack shrugged.

"And how are you going to get back to Bethel?"

A slow smile covered Jack's face, his eyes peaceful for the first time in a long time. "Don't you worry about that. I'm still gonna be here for a while. I'll find a ride home."

"Are you sure?" Christian asked, desperation peppered his voice.

"Yeah, man, go and get your girl."

"Thank you. I owe you one." Frantically dashing around the room, Christian gathered his stuff. Neatness and folding could wait. He needed to get on the road.

A half hour later, Christian was ready to go. Anything he'd left Jack could bring back when he eventually returned to Bethel.

"Go get her, man." Jack gave him a hard thump to his back.

A few hours and he would be with Willow.

"You're looking much better this morning." Willow's mom stepped into the room.

"I feel much better, but I've forgotten a lot. Haven't I?"

Her mother looked stunned for a second then asked, "How did you know?"

Willow pointed to the book on the bedside table. "It says May."

Her mother pulled the blue chair closer and took a seat. "I don't know what the nurse told you yesterday, but you've been in a coma for almost four months, and you have no memory as far as we can tell of the two weeks before the accident. Dr. Thompson said there is a possibility that you'll regain those memories someday, but you might not." She let out a long exhale.

There was a faint knock at the door, then the door swung open. Willow's breath caught in her chest, her lips lifting into a smile as a familiar face entered the room. Christian.

For what seemed like an eternity, they stared at each other.

Then a smile broke out on Christian's face. "Willow, you're awake." The way he said her name was almost like a caress. Christian took two quick steps to her bedside, his hands reaching out to hers.

What was going on here? Why did she feel like all the air had been stripped from her lungs, like her heart would jump out of her chest at any moment?

"Christian," her mother said, "there's something we need to talk about." She tapped the chair beside hers.

With obvious reluctance, Christian let go of Willow's hands and went to sit by her mom, but his gaze stayed focused on her.

"Willow has some memory loss. She doesn't remember the accident or around two weeks before that."

Christian's eyes widened. "You mean . . . "

"The last thing I remember is being pushed back from the cliff," Willow said.

Christian slowly blinked then swallowed. His euphoric expression crashed into something sad and filled with disbelief and longing.

"I'll leave you two alone to talk," her mother said at last and excused herself from the room.

"It's okay," Christian said. "I guess I'll just have to win you over again." His brown eyes watched her, full of love, and yet it didn't scare her like she'd expected it would. Instead, it warmed her, filling her with joy.

"But that's the thing, Christian, I do feel something for you. I feel like I should feel the way you do, but I have no memory of it. No memory of us." Anxiety raced through her veins, wet droplets falling on her white comforter. She gasped for breath then dissolved into tears. In an instant, strong arms were around her. Arms that brought comfort and security. Arms that she knew would hold her for as long as she needed without asking anything in return.

Sweet words whispered in a soft baritone washed over her. Christian was praying for her. Clinging tightly to him, Willow walked through her memories. There was Pastor George and then there was Christian on his knees in prayer. Her mind raced through the party at Amy's, cringing at the images before it stopped. "God loved you enough to save you, Willow." The words sung with certainty in her spirit, another piece of the puzzle falling into place.

Christian pulled back and looked at her, his gaze intense.

"What is it?" she asked, reaching for him again.

Christian sighed, taking her hands and holding them away from him. "I keep waiting for it to happen. For you to change back to the old Willow and this all to have been a dream. What if you never regain your memory? Will the feeling of remembered love be enough?"

In that moment, Willow understood what Christian was asking. Would there still be a *them* when all of this was over? Her heart beat faster in her chest. She loved him. She didn't know how or why, but she knew she did.

Leaning forward, she wrapped her arms tightly around his waist. "I love you, Christian. Not a remembered love, but a love that beats so loud and hard in me that I can't see anything else."

Christian's body shuddered against hers. "I missed you so much," he whispered, pressing his lips to her forehead. "There were days that I lost hope you would ever come back to me. That I would never see your eyes open again."

She smiled and tipped her head back, lifting her face toward him. Her recovery might be a long one, but she knew that with God and with Christian, she could make it. "I'm here now. Here with you."

EPILOGUE

Christian turned into Willow's driveway. White snow blanketed the trees outside, reflecting the bright light of the moon. Winter really was beautiful. Taking a deep calming breath, he climbed out of the car and straightened his tie, sliding his shaking hands into his pockets. His stomach clenched in a hard knot of anxiety. He quickly checked the side mirror to make sure he was still presentable.

He stumbled up the ice-covered steps, catching himself on the door handle before he landed on his face.

"Very suave, Christian," he muttered to himself. Taking another deep inhale, he rang the doorbell. The tingle of a thousand little bells rang just beyond the door.

Anxiety rippled through him. *Stop it, she's going to be happy to see you*, he told himself. The door swung open and a gasp escaped him. Willow stood before him, smiling shyly. Her gorgeous brown hair hung in soft beach curls, and she wore a deep blue A-line dress that rested just above her knees. Her pink lips pulled upward in a delighted smile.

"Christian," she said.

Her voice broke him out of his stunned silence. His arms slipped around her waist, and his lips found there way to hers. He kissed her with all the pent-up longing he'd endured these past months away at college.

After a long moment, Willow pulled away. "I take it you missed me?" A gentle light twinkled in her eyes. "I have the best news."

"Yeah?" He caught her around the waist and pressed his lips to hers again.

Willow pushed him back, her cheeks flushing. "Wait, wait. I can't think when you're doing that."

Christian grinned. "Good. Then you won't mind if I do it again."

With a firm hand on his shoulders, Willow stepped out of his arms. He stepped forward, and Willow took another few steps back. "You keep your kissable lips to yourself until I'm finished talking okay."

"I can't promise that, but I promise to try." He tried to fake an innocent expression, and he must've succeeded because Willow took a step forward.

"Well, you know how I finally finished high school?" She took another step forward. "I've decided to go to college! I'm coming with you after Christmas break!" She jumped forward and hugged him.

Christian felt his anxiety ease, her words making the plans he'd been holding close to his chest come to life. No one except Mr. Rysen knew what he'd had in mind tonight. Turning her face up to his, he kissed her long and slow, love for her overtaking him.

Taking his hand from her waist, he slid it into his back pocket. Now was the time. Staying focused on Willow, he went down on one knee and lifted the trembling box up between them.

"Willow, I know our relationship has been an abnormal one from the first time you knew I existed on the planet." Willow giggled and flushed. "But since that day in the school library, I've know that you are the one for me. I don't want to have to go back to college alone, I want you by my side every day and every night for the rest of my life. Please, will you be my love, my roommate, and my wife? Will you marry me?" The last word was almost a whisper as emotion overcame him.

Willow's eyes glittered with tears, and she nodded.

"Is that a yes?" He jumped to his feet.

"Yes," she gasped. "Yes, I want to marry you!"

Her lips crashed into his, their passionate kiss intermingled with tears. Breaking the kiss, Christian slid the ring onto her finger. "Forever."

"Forever."

ACKNOWLEDGMENTS

I would like to thank God for giving me this wonderful chance to spread His love through fiction. I would also like to thank my husband for his love and unfailing support through many hours of writing and editing. I would also like to thank my editor Megan Gerig for all her hard work and dedication during the editing process and the encouragement and support she gave me. And the people at Ambassador International for giving me the opportunity to minister in this way.

SOMEONE
LIKE
YOU
MICHELLE DYKMAN
BETHEL PRIVATE SCHOOL SERIES | BOOK TWO

Candice Hillman is on the precipice of completing her senior year at Bethel Private School. Although her parents are mostly absent from her life after their divorce, Candice finds support in her housekeeper, Mrs. Potter, and her boyfriend Brad. When a night of too much partying leads to a pregnancy, her carefully-constructed world comes crashing down forcing Candice to relook at her life and the choices she makes regarding her baby.

Someone Like You is a heartfelt look at the struggles of teenage pregnancy and takes readers on a journey of acceptance, forgiveness, and the wonders of God's grace with a little bit of romance thrown in along the way.

For more information about
Michelle Dykman
and
You, Me, and the Stars
please visit:

www.michelledykman.com

For more information about
AMBASSADOR INTERNATIONAL
please visit:

www.ambassador-international.com

Thank you for reading this book. Please consider leaving us a review on your favorite retailer's website, Goodreads or Bookbub, or our website.

Kate Sullivan will stop at nothing to find the man she holds responsible for her sister's death, and movie director Chris Johnston has information she needs. To get the answers she seeks, Kate joins his new production company, but when revenge and love collide, both Kate and Chris get more than they bargained for.

All Karrie wants is to fit in, but growing up in an alcoholic and abusive home does not make that easy. Her struggles take up most of her energy, and while her church seems to be aware of the violence in her home life, they are uncertain as to what actions they should take. When she is removed from the only life she has ever known, she feels as if her life will unravel as she tries to hang on to her Christian faith in the foster care system . . .

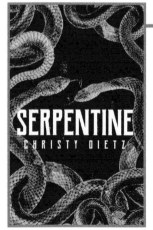

Determined to survive, an orphaned Esther must fight a rising new order in a broken America. This new order, the Federation of Acceptance, enforces directives that jeopardize human rights and beliefs. Esther must decide where she stands as she faces disappearing teachers, murdered classmates, and a traitorous ex-flame. Haunted by the mistakes of her parents' past, Esther is forced to make decisions that will affect the lives of everyone around her.